Seeds of Chaos
-Eden's Gate-

Herbert Grosshans

Published by
Melange Books, LLC
White Bear Lake, MN 55110
www.melange-books.com

ISBN 978-1-61235-018-9
Seeds of Chaos, Book One, Eden's Gate,
Copyright © 2006-2011 Herbert Grosshans

Credits
Editor – Taylor Evans
Format Editor – Mae Powers
Cover Layout: Mae Powers

Seeds of Chaos
-Eden's Gate-
by
Herbert Grosshans

Falsely accused of a crime, Commodore Thomas Reginald Stone's promising career is brought to an abrupt halt. Accompanied by two beautiful, oversexed alien women, he begins his search for the mystery planet that may provide the answer why someone wants him dead. However, trouble follows him wherever he goes.

* * * *

Herbert Grosshans is the Author of the Xandra series and numerous short stories. He discovered the wondrous world of Science Fiction as a teenager and wrote his first full-length novel 'The Galactics' before he was twenty. Written in German on an old typewriter long before computers and word processors became popular, it is still unpublished and will remain that way.

He writes his stories the old-fashioned way, with a pen in a scribbler, usually without an outline. Just an idea and maybe a couple of characters. As the characters come alive so does the story, and most of the time everything comes together in the end. Transferring the story into the computer is the first edit.

Aside from Science Fiction, he's tried his hand writing contemporary, mainly mystery thrillers. All of his stories contain erotica, but that may change in future novels.

Eden's Gate is Book One of Seeds of Chaos. Book Two, Hell's Gate, is available now.

Find out more on his blog http://hegro.blogspot.com

Seeds of Chaos
Book One: Eden's Gate
By
Herbert Grosshans

Chapter One

She had emerald eyes. They sparkled with bright iridescent colors behind extremely long eyelashes. She was not human. Not even of human stock. The planet she came from so far away from the known sector of Human space that I never heard of it…and she was the most beautiful creature I ever laid eyes on.

She laughed as I rolled away from her, gasping for breath. I've been known to brag about my sexual prowess, but this female just put me through an endurance test, and she didn't even breathe hard.

"You have good staying power," she said and moved on top of me. Her breasts were firm and round, jutting proudly from her solid ribcage. The long thick nipples brushed my lips as she lowered them into my face.

I didn't see a navel on her flat belly. Even though she had thick, luxurious bluish-black hair that hung down past her shoulders, her pubic area was completely smooth, and bare of any growth. Two strong bulging muscles framed her vulva, and she knew how to use them. There seemed to be no bone in her body, the way she writhed under and above me for the last couple of hours.

"I need a rest," I groaned and grabbed her undulating hips.

Her pearly teeth gleamed white in the pale light of the two moons and her laughter bubbled from red lips. "I am far from finished," she breathed and touched her lips to mine. I felt the tiny pinprick in my lower lip as she gently bit down and fed the aphrodisiac from her tooth into my bloodstream, a natural product, which the females of her species produced inside a special gland. It gave a male tremendous stamina and induced almost unbearably high orgasms.

Supposedly non-addictive, that's what she told me, but ever since I made love to her for the first time five days ago, I craved her body and nearness constantly. She had given herself to me completely. She even told me she loved me. How could I be sure? What did love really mean to her species? Before her, I hadn't even known women like her existed, not to mention the pleasure they could give.

I felt the strength flow back into my body, and with a loud groan, I pushed up against her. The incredible softness of her alien vagina closed around my hard penis, and I experienced instant pleasure. My eyes stared at the spot where we were joined, then traveled up her smooth, rippling belly, to her taut, softly jiggling breasts, to come to rest on her pale, beautiful face. Her warm, almost shy smile conveyed the impression of a gentle creature, which was a lie. Her emerald eyes sparkled with a wild, passionate fire, and her hips moved with fierce, powerful thrusts. I knew this was no gentle creature!

She rode me for a long time. Her strange eyes never left my face. When she cried out, "Now! Now..." I let go and watched her smile match the fierceness of her eyes. At that instant, she looked more beautiful than ever, and I wished this moment would never end.

She whimpered like a wounded animal, and when we were both spent, she collapsed on top of me, her breasts flattening against my chest. I put my arms around her and held her tight, loving her not only for the pleasure she just gave me, but also for shedding her inhibitions and letting me see a glimpse of her true self.

After awhile she stirred and kissed me gently. "I believe I have finally been satisfied," she said, then added, smiling, "For now." She got up and padded to the toilet facilities. "I'm going to take a shower," she called back over her shoulder.

Watching her smooth, round buttocks move enticingly, as she walked away, I again felt a soft stabbing in my loins. I lay back and listened to the gentle splashing of the water. I felt exhausted, but my mind seemed suddenly clear. The fog that enveloped my brain for these last few days had now been lifted. What the hell happened here? For five days I stayed cooped up with an alien woman I never saw before, and literally fucked out my brains.

Who is this woman? Why did she pick me?

I got up and looked at my reflection in the mirror surface of one of the walls. I saw a tall, well-muscled man in his early thirties (that's Terra-norm), with a rugged, handsome clean-shaven face (thanks to the long lasting depilating cream I used), and short dark-blond hair.

I looked at Thomas Stone, Commodore Thomas Reginald Stone of the Terran Space Navy, Special Forces. A sudden tick lifted the right corner of my reflection's mouth and I felt the bitter memory rush back into my mind. *Ex-Commodore* Thomas Reginald Stone. Dishonorably discharged from the Service because of treason. That was only one of the charges. Those bastards!They framed me, and then robbed me of my good name, my pension, my way of life, my future. In addition, they saw to it that no ship would ever hire me. I was blacklisted...a pariah.

That's how I ended up on Korillia, a forsaken, dead-end, backwater planet, where nobody knew me, and nobody really cared to know me. A place where cutthroats, pirates, and losers hung about. Where you kept your mouth shut and your hand close to your gun, knife, or whatever weapon you took a fancy to. A place where you didn't pick up a strange woman and spend five days in some expensive hotel-room that you couldn't really afford, fucking her until you dropped from exhaustion.

But I did exactly that. I watched her reflection as she came out of the bathroom. She looked stunning. She'd combed her hair and applied some make-up to her face, nipples, and pubic area. Coming up to me from behind, she put her arms around my chest. She stood almost as tall as I did.

"Hungry?" she asked, the gaze of her emerald eyes traveling down my body. She laughed throatily and touched my semi-erect member. I could feel myself respond to her soft touch.

"Who are you?" I asked between clenched teeth, fighting for control over my body.

"You know who I am," she answered softly, and began stroking me. "I am Sharina, the Flame. You know me better than any woman you have ever known...and I know you. For these last five days and nights we have explored each other's bodies with painstaking detail. I have given you such pleasure that has not been experienced by many human males. And you have satisfied my craving like no other male ever has, even males from my own species. You know me, Commodore Thomas Reginald Stone."

With sudden anger I pushed her hands away and turned around to face her. "How do you know my name? I never told anyone who I was, not even you!"

She stepped back, lifted her hands in a defensive gesture and smiled. "No need to get angry, Thomas." Her voice sounded soft, soothing. "I am not your enemy, I am a friend." Her alien eyes stared into mine. "My feelings for you are genuine, but I have left much unsaid, and I guess it's time to talk. I needed to be sure."

"To be sure of what?"

She reached for my hand. "Come, sit down beside me, and I will explain."

Reluctantly, I let her pull me to the bed. We sat close together, our bodies touching. The warmth of her flesh against mine and the feel of her satiny skin made my blood boil. I cupped my hand over one of her soft breasts and tried to push her onto her back.

"Who are you, Sharina?" My voice came out as a hoarse whisper. "What are you?"

She resisted and gently removed my hand from her breast. Then she kissed me. Her lips brushed against my ear. "I do love you, Thomas, remember that, whatever happens," she whispered and pulled away. "No more love-potions, I want you to be clearheaded when we talk."

Before she could speak again, the door to our suite sprung open and two large figures burst into our room. They carried weapons…big ugly Needlers, and they were pointed at us. Neither of the two were human. Humanoid, but definitely not human. Their glittering black eyes were set widely apart. Instead of a nose, they had skin flaps over long slits. They moved like gills with every breath they took. Wide, thick-lipped mouths exposed two long incisors. The hands that gripped the Needlers were long fingered and tipped with sharp, curved claws.

Thorans. Had I never heard of them, their appearance would have scared the hell out of me; but I knew their kind, and that should have scared me even more. Should have, but didn't. A coldness came over my mind. My body tensed, ready to spring into action.

Their bulky, over-muscled bodies moved with grace and swiftness. They moved in for the kill. These two were assassins.

In the mirror I saw Sharina lift her hands in the universal expression of surrender. "We have no quarrel with the Thorans," she said with a hysterical sounding voice. "Please, don't kill us."

"It is him we want," one of them growled, "not you."

"But you'll kill me anyway."

"We never leave witnesses," the other one rumbled. "You are in the wrong place."

"Too bad…for you," she said, and moved.

I've never seen anyone move so fast. One moment she stood with lifted hands by the mirror, the next she appeared beside one of the Thorans. Her hand touched his neck and the bulky figure tumbled to the ground. Beside him his partner fell at the same time. I blinked my eyes. Somehow, the light seemed to be playing tricks with my vision.

Sharina stood over one of the felled Thorans, like a naked avenger with flaming eyes. Beside her lay the other assassin, but above him crouched another female figure.

She straightened out and gave me a radiant smile. "Hello, Thomas," she said with Sharina's soft voice.

"Who are you?" I managed to say very smartly and put a pillow into my lap. "I didn't expect any visitors."

Sharina's double laughed and came closer. Sharina smiled and winked at me. "Meet my sister, Kabrina," she said. "You'll like her."

"We are identical twins," Kabrina said, "and we share everything with each other."

"Everything?" I repeated like a dumb parrot, starring at her suddenly jiggling, naked breasts. I hadn't even noticed her removing her top.

"Everything." Kabrina said with a throaty voice and began peeling off the bottom part of her tight body suit.

I stared at her and then at Sharina. "You just killed two men, and all you can think of is sex?" I protested.

Sharina shrugged her shapely shoulders. "Killing always turns us on, tremendously." She smiled and went to close the door. She looked down at the two corpses. "We'll have to get out of here," she said, "there isn't much time."

"Time enough," Kabrina breathed beside my ear and pushed me onto my back.

Dumbfounded, I watched her straddle me, and then I moaned involuntarily as her soft, velvety sheath closed over my aching member. She bent down and kissed me. I felt the tiny prick of her tooth in my lip. She was as passionate and wild as her sister, and soon I found myself lost in a world of ecstasy and raw lust. There were times when I thought Sharina replaced Kabrina on top of me, but I couldn't be sure, and I didn't care. When they were done with me, I lay there, totally exhausted. One of them, I didn't know who, gave me the antidote as she kissed me. My mind suddenly cleared.

"We'll have to move fast," both of them said at the same time. They looked at each other and smiled. "Poor Thomas here will get all confused," one said and tied a knot into her long black hair. She looked at me with her strange emerald eyes. "I am Kabrina, and I love you as much as Sharina."

I let out a strangled laugh. "Love!" I said with a hoarse voice. "You don't love me. You used me to satisfy a weird craving you seem to possess. You have fucked me, but you didn't love me."

Kabrina pouted. "Thomas, Thomas, such crude language," she crooned and put a finger over my lips. Her full naked breasts swung in front of my eyes like a pair of hypnotic pendulums. "You don't understand our species. When we inject a male with our love potion, we form a bond with him. We cannot help but love you, even after the potion wears off. Let us face it…you are stuck with us." She looked at Sharina and smiled. "Both of us."

I just groaned. *Well…congratulations Mr. Thomas Stone. You managed to get yourself into another fine-looking mess!*

"Come on, Thomas," Sharina said. "Let's get moving."

"My knees are shaky," I complained. "I need a rest."

"You Humans," Sharina threw up her hands. "You are so weak."

"Who wouldn't be?" I said. "After having sex with two women. I never did that before."

"No?" Kabrina laughed and looked at Sharina. "He really doesn't know."

"What don't I know?" I demanded.

"That you had sex with two women before." Kabrina smiled and touched my face, gently. "These last five days…it wasn't always Sharina you were with."

I looked at Sharina. She just smiled and shrugged her shoulders. "We share everything."

I flopped back onto the bed.

Chapter Two

The clerk at the front desk didn't even give us a second look. His bulging eyes were glued to a video screen. Sharina and Kabrina donned gray capes, which covered their shapely forms. Their beautiful faces were hidden inside the large hoods. Not that it mattered much, these Korillians were not famous for their mental swiftness.

Outside, a strong, icy wind greeted us. To make it even more pleasant, tiny ice-pebbles pelted our faces. When I looked at the distant mountains, I saw dark clouds being pushed toward the settlement by the force of the wind, signaling the coming of a snowstorm. I could smell the snow in the air. My two companions pulled their heavy capes tighter around their slim bodies, but it was only an instinctive gesture. Their formfitting body-suits, as well as mine, were quite efficient insulators against the damp cold.

We hurried across the deserted street. Dawn was just breaking. It seemed that nobody got up this early, unless they all preferred to stay indoors, as I would have liked to do. We walked toward a large vehicle parked on the other side. Sharina touched the locked door with her hand, and it slid open to reveal a lavish interior.

"Hurry," Kabrina said huskily and pushed me inside.

I sank into a plush seat. A cleverly concealed lighting bathed the interior with a bright, even light. In the rear were two bunks, one on top of the other, each wide enough for three slim people. I saw a table, cooking facilities, and a washbasin.

"Nice," I said. "And very cozy."

Sharina touched my cheek. "Make yourself comfortable, Thomas, we are going on a trip." Before she slipped through a thick curtain in the front, she smiled over her shoulder and said, "Someone has to drive this thing."

Kabrina undid her cape and let it slide to the floor. Shaking the knot out of her long black hair, she let it spill across her creamy shoulders. Her emerald eyes sparkled mischievously. "I like my hair loose. With Sharina driving you won't confuse us." She winked, "At least not for awhile." Gracefully, she sank into the other seat.

I could hear the soft humming of the power unit, as our vehicle began to move, the only indication. Magnetic stabilizers neutralized any rocky movements caused by the uneven surface of the road.

"Where are we going?" I asked after awhile, watching Kabrina with sleepy eyes. The warmth and the steady hum of the drive made me drowsy.

Kabrina's strange, glittering eyes were large. She seemed to watch me like a reptile watching a potential meal. When she saw me looking at her, she smiled. "We have to get off this forsaken planet...and fast. They won't give up."

"I liked it here," I said, "why can't they leave me alone." I opened my eyes. "Who are *they* anyway?"

Kabrina shrugged, still looking at me.

"You are so beautiful," I murmured sleepily. "Just like your sister."

"You want me?" she whispered, opening the top of her body suit. Her large, shapely breasts tumbled out. She stood up, moved toward me and sat in my lap. Her breasts hung in front of my face. I inhaled the heady fragrance of her body.

She laughed throatily and pulled my head toward her bosom. I buried my face between her soft breasts and inhaled deeply. I've always loved the smell of a woman, especially when she smelled as nice as Kabrina.

I lifted her up and carried her toward the bunks, and then I watched her as she peeled off her body suit. It didn't take long to remove mine. I moved on top of her. Her legs opened, and I slid my stiff penis into her moist, welcoming softness. We kissed hungrily, and again she injected me with her love-potion. I didn't need it, but it was part of her species' mating ritual. She met my powerful thrusts with equal force. Her lower body slammed up against mine, and when I climaxed she cried out and let her own juices flow.

I held her tight until we were both spent. "You are just so damn beautiful," I sobbed, trying to catch my breath.

She kissed me and gently she began to milk my penis. I responded quickly to her demands, and soon we were lost in another wave of ecstasy.

"You are something else," she gasped into my ear. "I've never met a male with such sexual prowess. Are you sure you are a human being? Maybe you are some kind of artificial creation...a sex-machine."

"My sex-drive has always been above average, and I keep my body in top physical condition," I answered hoarsely between deep breaths. I knew the next climax would come with mind-shattering force, but I wanted to enjoy her soft, warm, naked body as long as possible. Slamming deep into her, I added, "I am human, but you're not. You're alien."

"To you I am," she said fiercely and wrapped her long strong legs around me. "It is all relative. As far as I'm concerned…you are the alien."

The soft, velvety touch of her hot squeezing vagina brought me to the point of no return. With a roar I emptied myself into her. I had to stifle her cries of pleasure with my mouth. Then I collapsed on top of her, and soon I fell asleep in her cradling arms. Even though I was spent and satisfied, I did not sleep well. I dreamed and my dreams were quite lucid. I knew that I dreamed, but I also knew that it was more than that. I remembered…again.

* * * *

The ship that hung in space looked huge. A colony ship, carrying colonists. However, according to the information we received, the ship was transporting soldiers from a rebel colony on its way to one of the remote planets, where they were to be trained to invade and attack planetary systems of the Terran Empire. Maybe Terra herself.

Our sealed orders were clear: Search and Destroy. We had the ship on our screens. Weapon systems were on line, and ready to be activated. All that remained was my command. I hesitated. Something didn't smell right. I had a bad feeling about this.

"Stand by!" I told the gunners and turned to the communications officer. "Hail ship," I said.

A face materialized inside the C-cube.

"This is Commodore Stone of the Patrol Ship 'Barracuda'. Are you aware that you are in Terran Space?"

"I am Captain Harkis of the starship 'Hope', and I am well aware of our location, Commodore. We will only be in Terran Space for another couple of days. The capacitors are almost fully charged for the next jump. Our course was registered with nearby planetary systems, and we obtained clearance with Terran Immigration."

I studied his face, wrinkled and bleached from spending years in the confinement of spaceships. The eyes were clear and honest.

"Permission to board ship." I said casually.

He nodded. "Permission granted. We will open the hangar for you."

Accompanied by three troopers, I took a shuttle across to the huge ship. The hangar doors were open and our shuttle entered the bowels of the starship *Hope*. We had one hour. If my ship didn't hear from me before then the big ship would be destroyed. The three troopers and I would be among the casualties.

Captain Harkis was old. He smiled when we stepped out of the elevator onto the bridge.

"Welcome aboard, Commodore," he beamed and held out his hand in the age-old custom of Earth.

I took it, held it briefly. I looked around. The bridge looked simple and ancient, as ancient as Captain Harkis. A young woman stood at the communications desk. In the navigator's chair sat a man almost as old as the captain. He glanced briefly at us and turned back to his instruments. We saw no one else on the bridge. No signs of soldiers, or even guards.

"What's your cargo, Captain Harkis?" I asked. "And your destination?"

"We are carrying human colonists to their new home 'Crystallis' in the Cartelli System, just newly discovered."

"Anything else?"

"Livestock in embryonic form, seeds, machinery." The captain spread his hands. "But all this has been reported to the proper authorities. What is this all about? Is something wrong?"

I smiled at him. "Nothing. This is just a routine inspection. May I see the *coffins*?" I was referring to the refrigeration units in which the frozen bodies of the colonists lay in cryogenic sleep.

"I'd be delighted to give you a tour, Commodore."

As we rode the elevator to another deck, I asked, "How many colonists do you actually transport?"

"There are 10,000 colonists in suspension, 5,000 men and 5,000 women."

"No children?"

"There will be. In five years." The captain smiled when he saw my puzzled look. "We also have 10,000 embryos in storage. Again 5,000 females and 5,000 males. In five years each woman will be implanted with one embryo, two years later with another one."

"Why can't they just have their own children?" I asked.

"They can and they will. But this will increase the gene pool. We want to give them the best chance to survive and prosper on their new home." He smiled again. "Maybe I should say 'our home', because this is my last trip. I will retire on Crystallis, with my wife."

"Your wife?"

This time the captain grinned. "The communications officer." He shrugged. "I know, she seems too young for me, but I am physically in good shape. There are still many active years left in me." He winked. "I have a good supply of rejuvenating drugs on board."

I glanced at my watch. We had fifteen minutes left.

"May I call my ship?" I asked.

The image of my *Second-in-Command* filled the large ancient screen. He had an anxious look on his face. "Commodore?" he asked.

"We'll be home for supper." I smiled.

"Mother is waiting," he answered, then added, "Hurry home." He signed off. The anxious look never left his face.

Everything should have been fine. So why did I have this lump in my stomach?

I turned to the young woman at the communications desk, the captain's wife, as I now knew. "Is everything alright?" I asked.

She gave me a searching look. "We are not alone," she said.

"What do you mean 'we are not alone'?" I barked, then I held up a hand. "Sorry, I am used to knowing everything that goes on around me. What are you talking about?"

"There is another ship in the direction of the Malcom-System, about two parsecs from here. It appeared exactly 29 minutes ago. I thought you knew." Her voice sounded clear and crisp. Very professional. She also had a nice set of tits.

"No, I didn't know." Damn! Something was definitely wrong here.

"Have a pleasant trip," I said to Captain Harkis and nodded to this wife. "I wish you luck."

She smiled, and it made my loins pound. That lucky bastard. She was a pool of fire and passion. One day she would kill him, that was certain. What a way to go.

Lt. Newcombe, my *Second-in-command*, did not smile when I entered the bridge.

"What's wrong?" I demanded.

He handed me a personal message recorder. "This came in twenty minutes ago."

I turned it on. There was no picture, just a voice. "Commodore Stone," it said harshly. "You have your orders. Execute!"

"Fuck you!" I told the voice and looked at the lieutenant. "They're colonists…that's all. Somebody fucked up somewhere. We

14

abort this mission. I take full responsibility."

We were exactly fifteen minutes away when our screen flared up.

My communications officer turned to me, his face stony, uncaring, but his eyes showed the shock he felt. "They destroyed it," he whispered hoarsely. "Why?"

"Did you ID that ship?" My voice sounded strange in my own ears. Twenty thousand innocent souls wiped out at the touch of a button. Ten thousand unborn, Ten thousand living…no, Ten thousand and three. Captain Harkis would not have to worry about taking his rejuvenating drugs. His beautiful young wife would not be able to kill him with her passion and love, after all. Unlucky bastard.

"Can you identify that ship?" I asked again.

"No, sir," came the communications officer's voice. "It came up so fast. Never seen anything like it. No markings, but certainly not one of ours."

"Colonial?"

"No, sir, they don't have the technology." He shrugged when I stared at him. "As far as I know."

"Relax." I told him. "Let's have a look."

I studied the recorded image of the black, delta shaped ship as it came closer, and a cold shiver ran down my spine. I'd seen it before, or one just like it. I did not recognize the signature of the weapon that they used, nor did we have anything like it in the computer's memory. It was powerful, the colonists never stood a chance. As fast as the mystery ship appeared, that's how fast it was gone. The last image I had on the screen was the brilliant new sun, and then nothing.

* * * *

I woke up, sweating, but cold. One of the girls seemed busy at the counter. I smelled food. She looked at me and smiled. "Hungry?"

I swung my legs off the bed, still shivering.

"For food," I said and grinned weakly.

She shook her long hair and laughed throatily. "You should feel rested. You slept for almost six hours. Kabrina is at the wheel, so you know what I want when you've eaten."

Chapter Three

Sharina…the Flame. She was named appropriately. The fire of her passion burned deep and hot. Lucky for me I rested and double lucky that I have great recuperating powers. She demanded my full attention. I hammered between her spread hot thighs for a full hour. Her cries of pleasure filled the interior of the vehicle and my own grunts were equally loud.

After I climaxed inside her clutching creamy vessel, she climbed on top of me and rode me for what seemed like hours, giving me unbelievable pleasure. I lost count of the number of orgasms she experienced, but when she came, she went wild, whimpered loudly and swallowed my hard member deep into her. She finally collapsed on top of me, her long black hair spilling over my face, she lay panting in my arms. After awhile she propped herself up on her elbows and smiled down at me. I studied her delicate lovely face, her nose, her red full lips, her white perfect pearls of teeth.

"So beautiful," I said and looked into her strange emerald eyes. Not human, I reminded myself. Her eyes are not human. She is not human.

Those eyes seemed to look deep into my soul. "What are you thinking, Thomas?" she asked.

I chuckled and pushed her off. "I am thinking how lucky I am."

"Lucky?" She lay on her back, her breasts jutting up, and her legs slightly apart.

I cupped one of her breasts. "Yeah, lucky. Lucky I am in such good shape. I'd already be dead otherwise."

She laughed and moved my hand down her smooth belly. Then she clamped her thighs over it. They were incredibly strong, her smooth thighs felt like a vice around my hand.

"Enough, Sharina!" I said, maybe a little too harshly.

She pouted and released my hand.

"Thomas," she said after awhile. "You are a strange creature." Her eyes were large and almost glowing as she studied me.

"No stranger than you to me." I answered.

"Not like that. You are different from other humans I know." She lay slightly on top of me. I could feel the softness of her breast as it flattened against my chest. Her pubis rubbed against my thigh. "You seem to have developed immunity against my injections."

16

So she had noticed.

"Does it matter?" I stroked her smooth buttock. She trembled slightly under my touch. Her breath washed warm and sweet over my face.

"I begin to wonder what other abilities you possess."

"What do you mean?" I rolled on top of her, her legs spread automatically. She gasped when I entered her.

"This," she moaned and moved against me. "I should be in control, not you."

I closed her mouth with my lips. Her long tongue snaked between my teeth, and whimpering she bucked beneath me. It didn't take long until I climaxed. She lay silent and unmoving when I got up.

"You are a bastard," she said softly, but she smiled when I looked at her.

I dressed and joined Kabrina in the front of vehicle. She chuckled when I sank into the seat beside her. "You two sure made a racket back there. I hope you left some of that energy for me."

"Is that all you think of...sex?" I said, trying to look stern.

She laughed. "Most of the time."

I noticed that we weren't moving very fast. The weather outside had turned quite nasty. Sleet and snowflakes were pelting the windshield and visibility almost zero.

"How can you see where we are going?"

"I can't. But we have very good navigational equipment." She pointed to the instrument panel and at the softly glowing computer screens. "This vehicle practically runs itself."

"I see." I settled back into my seat and watched the white large flakes hit the warm glass, melt and evaporate. I tried to make out the surrounding landscape, but found it impossible. Everything looked white. Glancing at my watch, I noticed it was late afternoon. We had been traveling for about eleven hours.

"Where are we?" I asked.

Kabrina studied one of the screens, a road map, but it didn't mean anything to me. "We are about 600 kilometers east of Rangir. Another 200 kilometers, and we'll be turning north."

"Where to?"

"Tagnaroc. If everything goes well we should arrive there tomorrow night."

"What's in Tagnaroc?"

She shrugged. "Friends...and a spaceship."

Probably a smuggler, I thought, but kept quiet. I didn't know too much about Korillia. This planet did not appear on tourist maps. The only ships that visited here where freighters with questionable cargo. Smugglers who wanted to trade their wares for other illegal contraband and passenger ships that brought mercenaries, fortune hunters, criminals, and losers.

I'm talking about the main spaceport. Who knew what kind of people preferred not to dock there. Hell…I might even fit in with them. Staring at the swirling snow felt quite relaxing and I began to see shapes and images.

* * * *

One year past by, but I remembered everything with crystal clarity. After pursuing a pirate ship for days it dropped into normal space, trying to shake us. The system was unknown, not marked on any maps. We had nothing in the computer.

A small sun with only five planets, the second one populated, but we never got a chance to land. The pirate entered the planet's atmosphere. When we tried to follow, three black delta shaped objects came streaking toward us from the direction of one of the two satellites. Our screen came alive. There were no visual images, just voice transmission.

"This sector of space is off limits to you!" The voice sounded harsh and hostile. "Leave at once!"

"This is Commodore Stone of the Terran Space Force. We are in pursuit of a criminal. Please identify this planet."

"Leave at once, or we will open fire!"

"Nice people," one of my officers mumbled. I agreed, but I shot him a warning glance.

"They are charging weapons," my communication officer advised me.

"Let's get out of here," I ordered, watching the three black ships come closer.

Then the sun darkened as we jumped into warped space.

* * * *

They didn't follow us and I wondered why. Especially since somebody tried to get rid of me now. I chuckled to myself and saw Kabrina giving me a sidelong glance.

"Something funny?" she asked.

Before I could answer, our vehicle came to a dead stop. Kabrina opened the door and stepped outside. A cold blast of air entered the cabin. She came back moments later, her hair covered with wet snow. "Huge snowdrift across the road." She hugged herself, shivering. "And it's freezing out there."

"So what now?" I asked.

"We could wait for them to plow the road, but I don't think that's a good idea." She gave me a steamy look through lowered lashes. "Then again…Sharina and I could keep you from getting bored."

"That I believe," I growled, "but I don't think so."

"Thomas, Thomas," Kabrina said in a husky voice. She leaned over and brushed my lips with hers. "I don't think you will ever understand our species," she whispered into my ear. "No male can stand up to us for long once he's tasted our body."

Again, she pressed her lips to mine and I steeled myself against the flow of her poison, but it didn't come. She released me and smiled. Her two needle-sharp fangs gleamed dully. "Not now," she said regretfully, and nodded to her sister who stuck her head through the curtain.

"Thomas here does not believe that we could fuck him to death if we put our mind to it, and he would do it gladly."

Sharina laughed. "He might surprise us. He is the most virile male I ever encountered. You may also have noticed that he doesn't respond well to our injections anymore." Then she became serious. "I've checked our location on the map. There is a fishing village about fifteen kilometers to the east. We could make it there on foot."

Kabrina agreed. "It will be dark in three hours. We should leave right away."

"I have already notified our friends. Someone will be waiting there for us." Sharina stepped back, and we followed her through the curtain.

The vehicle was well equipped for emergencies. We donned insulated outdoor suits and heavy boots. The boots were laced with heating coils, which were powered by tiny, but powerful cells.

"Looks like you girls planned this well," I remarked. Sharina chuckled.

"We leave nothing to chance, Thomas," she said. "We are professionals in more ways than one."

A lot of snow fell and the high winds blew huge snowdrifts. I foresaw a grueling trek ahead of us.

After checking her compass Sharina began walking eastward. We sank up to our knees into the snow, and the going proved slow and tedious. Fortunately, the wind blew from the north, and if I held my head a bit in an angle I could keep the wind out of my face. The two girls were only a couple of meters in front of me, but in the driving snow they looked like two ghostly shadows. We could easily be separated and never find each other, but they took precautions even against that. A strong rope clicked onto our belts kept us connected.

The snow became packed in places, and you could walk on top of the hard but treacherous crust. You never knew when you would break through, and it happened more often than not. It seemed the wind became stronger since we left the vehicle, and I wished we had waited the storm out in the comfort of the warm camper. We could have rested and slept peacefully. I knew, of course, that there would not have been much rest for me, not with those two oversexed vixens. A stupid phrase popped into my mind: I would rather fuck than freeze. Exhausting, yes, but much more pleasurable than this.

I cursed as my right foot disappeared again, throwing me off balance and sending me for a dip into the deep snow. As I struggled back onto my feet, the rope that connected me to one of the girls tightened. The shadow in front of me stopped and waited until I stood upright again. I took a step and sank back in. Since I weighed more than the girls, I broke through the crust much more often.

"I need a rest!" I yelled into the wind and tucked on the rope.

Sharina and Kabrina came back and squatted down beside me.

"I need to rest for awhile," I repeated. They nodded and huddled close to me. "We should find some better shelter," one of the girls said, "I don't think we are going to make the village today. It will be dark soon, and we'll have to spend the night."

Not that getting dark would make that much of a difference. We couldn't see anything in this blizzard anyway.

"How far have we come?" I asked.

Kabrina consulted one of the electronic devices she carried strapped to her left arm. "Not far," she said, "about four kilometers in two hours."

"Another two kilometers and we should get into the forest. We'll find protection there." Sharina stood up. "Let's get moving."

The short rest and the booster pills we swallowed restored our energy and we made better progress than before. It was dark when we finally entered the anticipated forest. The trees had thick trunks with rough bark and wide branches, and they didn't crowd each other. Between them grew short underbrush. Fortunately, it presented no problem to us. Snow still covered the ground, but not as much, and the force of the wind seemed considerably weaker.

The deeper we entered into the forest, the better it became.

Kabrina, who provided the lead, switched on a light, which she clipped to the buckle of her belt. In its powerful beam we could see quite well.

After stumbling through the trees for another half hour, we suddenly came across a narrow road. It led eastward, so we followed it. Walking became much better, even though it would have been impossible to travel it with a larger ground vehicle in this deep snow.

Sharina, who carried a light in her hand, swept the sides of the road periodically. I didn't much attention, being much too busy contemplating my recent situation, when my cheery thoughts were interrupted by a loud whoop from her.

Looking up, I let my gaze follow the beam of her torch light. I could have 'whooped' myself at the wonderful sight. A cabin. Shelter for the night. It was enough to cheer up anyone.

We approached it carefully. Kabrina knocked with her fist against the door, but we didn't get an answer. When she pushed at the heavy wooden door, it swung open. After shining the light into the interior, it became quite evident that this place was abandoned. We entered, still cautious, but discovered nothing in the cabin but emptiness.

In one large room stood a stone fireplace. There were two more rooms in the back, one with a wide bunk in it, obviously a bedroom, the other one clearly the kitchen. It had an old rusted iron stove for cooking, a wooden counter with some pots on it and a crude table with four chairs in need of repair.

"It's not much," Sharina chuckled, "but it's home."

We went back into the room with the fireplace and found a pile of wood stacked in one of the corners. I put some into the fireplace. Sharina handed me a small torch. I carefully lit a few kindling, fed the tiny flames for a while, and before long we had a nice, crackling fire going. I sat in front of it, staring into the flames and enjoying the warmth on my face. The girls lay curled up on either side of me, and it could have been a very romantic evening...under different circumstances.

Chapter Four

"Commodore Stone, why did you destroy that ship full of colonists?" The deep, resonant voice of Admiral Sasmussen asked me again. I've never liked that man. There was something about him that I couldn't put my finger on. Tall and skinny, with a haggard and gaunt looking face, his dark eyes seemed to burrow right into my skull, and his voice sounded like the voice of doom.

And in my case, it certainly was. This man wanted to bury me.

His constant badgering failed to intimidate me and I was getting angry. "Sir, as the record shows, it was not my ship that fired, even though we had sealed orders to destroy that ship. I am guilty of disobeying orders, nothing else."

Admiral Sasmussen shook his head. "Commodore Stone, when are you going to stop this charade? I have a record of your orders right in front of me. You were supposed to carry out a routine inspection of the starship 'Hope' and to ensure that the ship would leave in the designated time-span. No mention of destroying it." He smiled. An executioner looked friendlier. "I signed those orders myself."

I shrugged. "Then those records are false." I said and knew how he would answer. We had been through this before.

The admiral stood up and pounded both fists on the desk. "Are you accusing me of lying, Commodore?"

"No, sir, I would never do that." I stayed cool even though I wanted to wring his scrawny neck. "I am only stating the facts as they happened and as I know them. My crew is witness."

"Your crew?" he barked. "How convenient! There is no one left."

"That's right!" It was my turn to bark. "How convenient. I demand an investigation why every member of my crew happened to be on the same cruise ship at the same time. And why that same cruiser collided with a rogue asteroid."

"Do not raise your voice in my courtroom again!" Admiral Sasmussen's voice dropped dangerously low. "I have a good mind to have you executed immediately. But you have friends." He gave Admiral Curtis a sour look.

Admiral Curtis, who sat beside him, said nothing. He kept looking at me, his face unreadable. He was my superior, but he was more than that, much more.

His wife, Elesia Stone-Curtis, was my adopted mother. That made him my stepfather.

"Let me give you the real facts, Commodore Thomas Reginald Stone." The voice of Admiral Sasmussen dripped with sarcasm. "Even though you had no orders to do so, you took it upon yourself to destroy the starship 'Hope', which carried 10,000 colonists in deep stasis. Ten thousand people who dreamed of a better life on a frontier planet, where they could live in peace, raise their children, and grow their own food. Ten thousand lives that you destroyed with your unspeakable act of playing god. This act brought us to the brink of war with the colonies. You claim that you had orders to destroy the ship, but you disobeyed those orders. Then an unknown ship came out of nowhere and fired the lethal shots. A ship which you had seen before on another mission ten months ago, when, after pursuing a pirate ship, you dropped into an unknown system." He looked up and stared at me. "You insist on keeping this story alive and yet…there is no record of that mission, and there is no record of any mystery ship. There are no records, Commodore Stone, not in the Fleet's computers, nor in your own ship's computer! And computers don't lie."

"The computers don't lie, but the people who program and maintain them do." I kept my voice low and calm, even though I boiled inside. "I don't know what is going on, but somebody is trying to sweep something under the rug and me with it, and I will lead my own investigation to find out why."

"There will be no investigation, at least none you will head, Commodore. I recommend your dishonorable discharge from the Service. You will be stripped of your rank and privileges!" Admiral Sasmussen spoke coldly. His eyes could have frozen Hell itself. "And if you insist on pursuing your conspiracy theories I will personally see to it that you end up on some hell-hole of prison planet for the rest of your life…"

Your life…your life…

* * * *

The voice boomed around inside my head, and I shivered, despite the heat from the fireplace.

I became aware of a pair of hands fumbling with the belt around my waist. "It's warm enough in here now," a voice whispered into my ear, "let's get undressed and create some of our own heat."

Sharina put her mouth on mine, and then I felt the sharp prick in my lip. Fire raced through my veins, and I let it happen.

She was already naked, and it didn't take long before my own clothes were piled up beside hers. With a loud groan I rolled between her welcoming open thighs, and then we were locked together. The soft, creamy walls of her alien vagina closed around my aching shaft.

Another pair of gentle hands stroked my back, and after my first climax Kabrina took her sister's place under me. She moved just as passionate, whipping her lower body with great enthusiasm. She cried out and scratched my back as we both experienced a tremendous orgasm.

Then they made me lie on my back and took turns riding me. They were insatiable, and so was I. After awhile I couldn't tell anymore who writhed on top of me. Both girls had let their hair down, and both were equally passionate and wild.

The flickering flames of the fire threw shadows and golden light over their moving bodies. My eyes were glued to a pair of up-tilted breasts as they bopped up and down. Then the long nipple of another breast thrust into my mouth and a mass of black hair spilled over my chest.

There were only glowing embers in he fireplace by the time they were finished with me.

I lay on my stomach, watching one of the girls add some more logs and stoke the fire. She lifted up her beautiful ass as she bent to blow into the flames, and I quickly moved behind her, grabbed her smooth hips and pushed my erect member between those lovely cheeks. She gasped as I slid into her soft sex-canal and pushed her round buttocks higher up for deeper entry.

"You sly devil," she cried out and steadied herself against the hearth. "I thought you were exhausted."

"I recuperate fast," I grunted and snapped my pelvis furiously back and forth. When I climaxed inside her, she doused my pumping member with her own love-juice. Then she collapsed under me. "My legs are weak," she complaint, but smiled.

"What about me?" a voice came from behind me. Searching soft fingers closed around my half-erect penis. She laughed delightedly as her touch brought an immediate reaction. She moved away, and I turned to watch her get to her knees. Pointing to her round buttocks, she crooned, "I want the same as Sharina."

Kneeling behind her, I spread her golden cheeks and put my glans between her swollen lips. Very slowly I entered her and buried my penis to the root. Then I grasped her breasts and began to move in and out of her clutching vagina. This time I didn't hurry. She whimpered and clawed at the furs as I slowly and methodically brought her from one orgasm to another. She finally slid to the floor, and I cradled her under me, still inside her. "I am totally exhausted," she panted. "You can't be human, Thomas, no matter what you say."

I laughed and pulled out of her. "Maybe you've underestimated the human males. We are not all the same, you know."

The fire crackled, and outside the storm still raged furiously. I lay on my back, the girls snuggling close to me on each side. The fragrance of their perfumed hair tickled my nose, and it smelled good. We were all still naked. Their soft bodies felt warm and silky against my skin, and I held them tight against me.

Moments like that are to be cherished. They don't come along every day.

Kabrina found another reasonably clean fur in the other room and threw it over us. And with the fire burning it felt quite comfortable in the cabin.

Even though I was tired, I had troubles falling asleep. Beside me the girls were breathing softly and regularly. They seemed to feel secure in my arms.

Who were these girls? Why were they here, and what did they want from me? They both claimed to be in love with me, but somehow I didn't buy it. They acted like a couple of sex-starved nymphomaniacs and seemed to enjoy, even crave, our sexual encounters, as I did, I must admit.

But I had no ulterior motive. I just like fucking, and when the opportunity presents itself, I will take it. Not that I cannot go without it for a long time. I can adapt to any situation very quickly, that's what made me such a good soldier. That's why I had risen to rank of Commodore in a short time, and that's why I had been a member of a Special Elite Team.

Another question I asked myself.

Who was I? What was I?

I am a foundling. A team of researchers found me living among a tribe of aborigines on one of the planets in the *Altair System,* naked and filthy. I had no memory of my natural parents. There were no other humans living on that planet. I was either the lone survivor of a crashed space ship or the abandoned reject of a slave trader. I spoke only the language of the aborigines, which consisted mainly of grunts and gestures.

The head of the team, Prof. Elisia Stone, took a liking to me and began to educate me. With the help of computers, I learned the Terran language very quickly and everything else they crammed into my head. A year later Elisia Stone adopted me as her son and a year after that she married Admiral Curtis.

The Admiral and I became good friends. He was like a father to me. He recommended I join the Space-force, because he saw potential in me. I rose very quickly in the ranks, and not just because of my connection to Admiral Curtis.

As I said, I adapt.

I became Commodore Thomas Reginald Stone, until two months ago. Now I was just plain Thomas Reginald Stone, private citizen. A man without a future. A man that somebody wanted dead. Might as well erase my memory of the last fifteen years and let me start fresh. It would be less painful. Drifting into an uneasy slumber, I dreamed about a beautiful golden-skinned man with golden wings.

* * * *

He smiled when he became aware of me.

"Everything ends," he said gently. Then he spread his wings and took to the air. He climbed higher and higher, until he touched the clouds. I watched him soar across the sky, a deep longing inside me cried out.

From my shoulders sprouted golden wings and with a shout of joy I leaped toward the sky. The clouds opened, revealing a huge gate. I looked upon a world filled with lights and happiness. The golden man entered the gate.

When I tried to follow the clouds darkened and a bolt of lightning hit me in the chest. As I tumbled toward the ground a voice like thunder rumbled through the black sky, "You cannot enter! You can never enter!"

The ground rushed up. I screamed and awoke.

* * * *

I felt gentle fingers on my lips. "Hush," whispered a soft voice. "You are only dreaming."

Two warm bodies were in my arms and I smiled. This was real. I closed my eyes again. Tomorrow would bring more trouble, but that was tomorrow.

Chapter Five

The storm weakened in the morning and the howling of the wind stopped. Only hot ashes remained in the fireplace, and the interior of the cabin turned cold. When I exhaled, my breath formed a ghostly mist.

Under the furs, the girls pressed their naked bodies against mine. "I'm freezing," one of them complained, "I need something warm inside me." Her hand touched my penis.

"So do I," said the other one, her teeth nibbling on my ear.

Right now sex was the last thing on my mind. "Girls, girls," I said. "Is that all you ever think of?"

"Most of the time," they both said in unison and laughed. "Don't you?"

Their laughter sounded so cheerful and sweet, it could have melted the coldest heart. I held them tight for a moment, and then I sat up with both of them still clinging to me. "I'm getting dressed, and I am also hungry," I declared and they both protested, pouting. "You are cruel, Thomas. We need sex everyday or we can't function."

I laughed and stood up. They slipped back under the furs and watched me getting dressed.

"He means it," one of them said.

"We are losing our touch," said the other one, and they both giggled. Then they threw their covers off and got up. Naked, they pranced around, stretching and going through some exercises. Again I marveled at their incredible beauty.

"I thought you girls were cold?" I remarked, trying to control my reacting body. Standing wide legged in front of me, one of them smiled. "I am Sharina, the Flame," she said. "I am always hot, and so is my sister. Our bodies adapt easily to our environment." She began tying back her black luxurious hair. "I notice you still can't tell us apart. Maybe this will help."

Kabrina struck a sexy pose in front of the fireplace. Looking at me with half closed lids, she purred, "Come, lover, share a few moments of ecstasy with me and my sister, before we leave here. Who knows when we'll have the opportunity again."

Looking at Sharina's strangely glittering emerald eyes, she reminded me again of her alien nature. Sharina lifted up and kissed

27

me full on the mouth. Then her hand touched my crotch. She laughed when she noticed my hard penis.

"There is still hope," she called to her sister and began to undo my belt. Then she pushed down my pants, and it wasn't long before I was completely naked again. Sharina pulled me down on top of her, her legs fell open and with a loud groan I slipped into her warm, welcoming moistness.

So much for willpower, I thought, as my body rocked between her wide-open thighs. Another pair of hands stroked my back, touched my buttocks, gently squeezing my scrotum. After my first climax I lay suddenly on my back, Sharina bouncing on top of me.

Then she lifted up, moved to the side, only to be replaced by her sister. Kabrina must have been going out of her mind watching us for so long. Her vagina felt hot and wet. She slipped it over my stiff mast and she cried out almost immediately as her body shook from a tremendous orgasm. I slammed up against her and watched her eyes blaze with fierce passion.

Even though it was cold, I began to sweat. This girl demanded all of my strength, and there wasn't much left. Sharina took most of it already.

I let her ride me for a while, enjoying the sight of her beautifully shaped breasts jiggling up and down. Then I pulled her toward me, rolled her onto her back and began to fuck her with furious strokes. Where I found the strength I don't know, but I lasted for a long time.

She pulled her knees up against her chest, allowing my shaft to pierce her deeply. Finally, she cried out, "Enough, Thomas, let it happen…now!" Her legs flew open as I climaxed. She lifted her lower body off the floor to meet my deep thrust. I lay still and clasped her to me, letting my fluid jet into her. I felt her response as her own floodgates opened.

I collapsed into her cradling arms, breathing hard and completely exhausted. With satisfaction, I noticed her ragged breathing and still body.

"That was absolutely beautiful," Sharina whispered hoarsely beside my ear. "Watching you two was an experience I totally enjoyed."

"Don't get any ideas," I groaned. "You had your turn."

She turned my head and kissed me hard. Then she stood up, laughing. "Don't worry, there is always tonight."

Kabrina stirred beneath me. "I didn't think it was possible," she said with a low, almost dreamy voice, "but you've managed to satisfy my craving, Thomas."

I pulled my limp member out of her and rolled onto my back. "So did you," I said. "But you two girls are going to kill me with your sexual demands. I don't know how long I can keep this up."

Sharina chuckled. "We'll give you a helping hand. You'll keep it up." She bent down and took my penis into her hand. Lifting it up, she laughed, "See."

Grinning, I put my hand behind her neck and pulled her down. She sprawled on top of me, her warm breasts against my chest. I could feel her body tremble, and when she kissed me she bit down, not too gently, she was too aroused for that. I didn't care, hot fire raced through my veins and my manhood responded. Her legs opened, she lifted up, and then her hot soft sheath slipped over my rigid mast.

"I told you," she breathed against my cheek and began to rotate her lower body furiously.

It didn't last long, but when I climaxed it happened again with mind-shattering force. I grabbed her quivering, soft buttocks with my hands and pulled her deep into my lap as I emptied myself into her.

She whimpered like a wounded animal and cried out in a strange language.

When we were both spent, we lay cradling each other, still locked together.

"What was that all about?" Kabrina said beside me. "I'm almost jealous."

Sharina disengaged herself from my embrace and sat up. "Lust, my dear sister," she smiled. "Total, unabashed lust. No need to be jealous."

I pulled the furs on top of me and lay there, completely exhausted. Watching the girls get dressed, I again admired their athletic, but smoothly muscled bodies. My eyes feasted on their beautifully shaped breasts, their narrow waists, flaring hips, and those lovely, shapely buttocks.

"Are all women on your planet as beautiful as you?" I asked.

Sharina looked at me with her large emerald eyes. "You really think we are beautiful, Thomas?" she queried, "Or is it just my love potion that clouds your eyes?"

"No," I answered truthfully, "you are truly beautiful. If I were an artist I would love to put the image of you on canvas over and over."

Kabrina laughed, but her eyes seemed thoughtful when she studied me. "That is sweet of you, Thomas." She came close and knelt beside me. "As I told you before, we are bound to you and we love you. Our bodies belong to you, and you can enjoy them whenever you want to." She bent down and kissed me on the lips. "But you better get up now. We have to get going."

Reluctantly, I climbed to my feet. One of the girls lit the fire again, and it felt comparatively warm inside the cabin. In the light of day the place looked even more desolate than under the cover of darkness.

"If you're looking for toilet facilities you won't find any." Sharina interpreted my searching look correctly.

"Probably outside." I nodded.

I dressed and went outside. The air smelled brisk and clear. A lot of snow had fallen overnight, but it looked soft and fluffy. It would be different once we left the forest, where the strong wind most likely blew the snow into huge drifts.

I found what I looked for and headed for it. The door hung on rusty hinges that protested with loud creaks when I forced it open. As expected, a seat with a hole in it. Not fancy, but functional. I also discovered a stack of faded printed sheets of paper nailed against the wall.

Smiling, I sat down. Somebody was spoiling me.

I didn't feel like hurrying, so I took my time, just sitting there, thinking. The dream from the night before came back to me. It had been so vivid.

Who was that golden-skinned man with the black wings? Nobody I remembered, unless it was someone from my life before I regained my memory. Probably not a real person at all…just a dream symbol, but what did it mean?

Chapter Six

The cold was creeping back into the exposed parts of my body. Time to go back to the warm cabin. Maybe the girls prepared something to eat. Who knew what they carried in their backpacks.

I rubbed my hands and face with snow and started back down the narrow trail. My built-in senses of danger told me something did not seem right. As I carefully stepped around to the front of the cabin, I noticed footprints in the snow around the doorway. They didn't seem to lead anywhere, as if, whoever made them, just dropped from the sky.

I groped for my gun.

Damn! I must have left it with my pack. I only had my combat knife strapped to my boot. Not much of a weapon against lasers.

Whoever came to visit didn't give me any time to ponder the situation.

The door flung open.

I stared at the figure confronting me. Obviously female, the slim body dressed in a tight outfit that clung to her like a second skin, and her full breasts didn't leave any doubt. A thin mask covered her face, but, from the eyes, I knew she was not human.

She stepped aside, bade me to enter with a fluid gesture of her long-fingered hand. Following her invitation I moved passed her into the room, my right hand hanging low alongside my body, fingers spread.

There were three more people in the room...two males, thick black capes hung from their broad shoulders, and a third one, yet of unknown gender. I only saw a tall and slim robed figure, the body and face hidden inside a loose hooded robe.

The robed one was the only one still wearing an anti-gravity belt. The others dropped theirs to the floor. Those devices were expensive, but not very reliable. Not even the military used them much.

The female, who invited me in, let the gaze of her large round eyes travel over my body. I sensed her smile behind the veil. "A handsome human specimen." She spoke in a soft, melodious voice. "I think I shall enjoy him."

"As we shall the two females," said one of the males.

I looked at the female, then at the males. I knew their species all

31

too well.

Flemlins.

The males were well known for their sexual prowess, as were the females for their powers of seduction. They talked with gentle voices, but that was deceptive. They were a fierce, wild race, and they could be cruel and vicious.

"We want your mates." The other male spoke up.

"They're not my mates," I said, "and not mine to give."

"They are with you," he stated. "We will compensate you."

"It is alright, Thomas."

I glanced at Sharina who spoke. "You know what they want?" I asked.

She smiled. "I do. They can help us to get out of here. Apparently, there are huge snowdrifts between here and our destination. They will lend us their belts."

I shrugged, watching the female walk toward me. She reached for my hand, and then she pulled me toward the entrance to the bedroom. Inside, she began to peel off her body suit. She had skin as white as the snow outside. Her body appeared flawless, with a tiny, almost too narrow waist, and slim hips, but her buttocks were round and firm, just like her breasts.

I had never seen females of her kind naked, and it surprised me to discover the thick thatch of pubic hair, pure white with a hint of purple.

When she stood naked, she came close, undid the upper part of my suit and pulled it over my head. Then she opened my pants, slid a slender hand down my belly. Her breath caught when she touched my already erect penis.

I didn't resist when she pulled my pants down to my ankles. I lifted my feet to step out of them. Something about her made me lightheaded and turned me on tremendously. Was it the way she smelled? The way she touched my body with her warm, long-fingered hands? I didn't know and didn't particularly care. All I knew, I wanted this female badly.

She took a few steps back, toward the bunk, and then she turned and bent. Her upper body rested on the bunk, her round buttocks were two pale globes beckoning to me. Her naked feet rested on the dusty floor. She looked back at me with her large dark purple eyes. I studied her beautiful body for a moment, noticed the long purplish hair that grew out of the nape of her neck and from her spine, like a soft brush.

Stepping behind her, I crouched over her. I felt the heat radiate from her slender body. My hard penis slid between her soft cheeks, and then with one hand I steadied myself on one of her buttocks, while the other one guided my mast through the thick mass of hair.

She pushed back, something soft and liquid grabbed my penis and then with a deep groan I felt myself slide into a hot inferno. Putting my hands around her narrow waist, I began pumping between those hot lovely cheeks. Even her body felt hot under my touch.

She milked my penis with great expertise, pushing her buttocks backwards every time I thrust forward.

The incredible softness of her truly alien vagina drove me into a frenzy and brought me almost unbearable pleasure. She seemed to sense when I was ready to explode. Her long fingers touched my scrotum, did something and the urge disappeared. But not the pleasure.

From the other room I could hear cries of ecstasy. I didn't have to guess what happened there.

The female in front of me stopped moving. "Pull out!" She spoke with a soft, but commanding voice. I obeyed, watched her straighten out. She took her cape and spread it on the floor, then she lay down on it, her legs spread wide.

I didn't need an invitation.

Cradled between her strong thighs, I let myself be guided to instant ecstasy. I cried out with a hoarse voice when I slid back into her creamy tight sheath. Her long arms went around my back, pulled my body against hers. The long, thick nipples of her soft breasts dug into my chest. I wanted to kiss her, but the mask still covered the lower part of her face. I had no idea what she looked like underneath that tight mask.

I felt the wave of pleasure washing through my body; it hit me with full force as I burst inside her. Long fingers dug painfully into my buttocks and strong arms pulled me deeper into her embrace. As I collapsed on top of her, I felt the soft touch of another pair of hands on my back. Turning my head, I saw the fourth member of the Flemlins kneeling beside us.

Another female.

Her naked breasts were almost touching my face.

"Come," she said with a soft and heavily accented voice. "You will serve me now."

She didn't look like the other one. Fine, dark purple fuzz covered her whole body. Only her hands, face, and breasts were free of it. Her skin was also purple, although of a lighter shade.

She wore no mask and the beauty of her face mesmerized me. Exquisitely formed, perfectly proportioned, but definitely not human. Her black eyes were round and large, the iris filling the entire socket, and the lashes were extremely long.

She smiled, displaying tiny white teeth. Then she lay down beside us. "Come," she said again.

The female underneath me released me. I moved over to the one beckoning to me, positioned myself between her widespread long legs. I looked down at the hairless sex-organ between them. Her thick labia were almost white, with just a purplish hue. I spread them with my fingers to expose the pink inside.

Then I lowered myself on top of her. Her large eyes locked with mine as I slowly pushed my hard penis into her soft creamy orifice. She was hot and liquid, just like the other female.

She let out a little gasp when I pushed deep, lunged up against me. At first she lay passive, let me do the work, then suddenly she threw her long legs around my back and began to writhe beneath me. I felt her alien vagina come alive, sucking and rippling along the length of my shaft.

Letting my mind relax, I became aware of only the sensations that raced through my body…the feel of her hot vagina sucking on my penis, the satiny fuzz of her soft fur warm and electrifying on my skin, the heady fragrance of her aroused alien body.

Her eyes were still locked with mine, her lips open, inviting. I crushed mine to hers. They were soft, warm and responsive. My tongue probed the inside of her mouth. She tasted strange, but pleasant.

Then I felt her vagina tighten around my shaft, felt the release of hot liquid. I had been ready to burst and took that as my cue. Without taking my mouth from hers I released the passion that built-up inside me and filled her with my own fluid.

When it was over, we separated. I lay on my back beside her, gasping for breath.

After awhile she turned, smiled and touched my cheek. "You are a surprise," she said with her melodic voice, and then she let out a series of chiming sounds, her version of laughter, I guessed. "But we are not finished," she said.

She stood up, searched for something on the floor and found what she was looking for…her anti-gravity belt. After strapping it around her narrow waist, she touched a button on its control panel.

Her body lifted into the air, floated toward me. Pulling up her knees, she hovered above my semi-erect penis. Again, she emitted her chiming laughter, and then she said something to the other female who sat beside me.

I felt a warm soft hand on my penis, then a barely undetectable sting in my scrotum. Something hot, almost like an electric shock, raced through my system. Between my legs my penis rose, became a hard, solid mast.

The female beside me let out a string of gurgling sounds; the other one laughed again and lowered herself onto my strutting penis. Once more, I entered instant bliss. She felt liquid and tight. Slowly, she began to rotate around my shaft.

I closed my eyes, just concentrated on the ecstasy spreading from my sex-organ throughout my whole body.

When she stopped I opened my eyes to watch her. She just hovered in the air, my penis deep inside her. Her large purple eyes locked with mine. Then she began to constrict her vagina walls with a steady rhythm. No other part of her body moved, except her incredibly liquid sex-organ.

Without a warning, she suddenly shot into the air, leaving my mast exposed and my highly overcharged system crying for release. Then the snow-white body of the other female floated above me, her arms and legs spread wide. I felt the soft touch as her pubic hair made contact with the swollen head of my penis.

For an agonizing moment she just hovered there, and then she dropped as if a rope lowered her. The soft heat of her tight sheath slipped over my shaft, engulfed it. Slowly she began to thrust her pelvis up and down, steadily increasing the speed.

I never felt the weight of her body. The only contact between our bodies the spot where we were joined. I closed my eyes, my mind aware only of that rippling, tight sheath of fire grabbing my penis. I felt like a volcano on the verge of eruption, but whatever potion they had pumped into me kept the eruption at bay for a long time.

They played me, taking turns.

When they tired of the game with the anti-gravity device, they knelt on the floor, side by side, their backs arched, their round buttocks raised. I took them from behind, first one, then the other one, moving back and forth between their white and purple buttocks.

After awhile they turned onto their backs, their knees bent and their thighs wide open. Again I moved from one to the other, sinking my pole into their alien vaginas, one hidden behind a thick bush of white hair, the other one hairless, white, between two purple, hairy satiny thighs, both equally soft, creamy, and alive.

The pleasure they gave me never stopped, until the raging inferno inside my loins couldn't be contained any longer.

The volcano erupted and spewed hot liquid into the eagerly receiving vessel.

At the height of my orgasm, I pulled out of the white female's vagina, and before I released another spurt, I sank deep into the purple female, just in time to douse her insides with my spermatic fluid.

She let out a surprised gurgle when I kept on gushing and pulled my mouth onto hers.

Then it was finally over.

Strength drained from me with a whoosh of air. Listening to my breath escaping my lungs, I lay there with my eyes closed, totally exhausted.

Chapter Seven

The female Flemlins lay on either side of me, their breathing fast and erratic. As my mind slowly entered a state of normalcy, a humorous, highly satisfying thought suddenly struck me. These two arrogant, over-sexed females had in all likelihood never met someone like me.

To be fair, the drug they injected into me was partially responsible for my performance, but only partially. I possessed a virility and stamina that most men only dream about.

I felt a soft, satiny arm on my naked chest. Opening my eyes, I looked into a pair of shiny black eyes. Even though the face and eyes of the female were alien, I could detect the dreamy look.

"Not even our own males can come close to your sexual prowess," she said softly. She bent to kiss me, but the kiss was not demanding and wild, but gentle, almost a lover's kiss. When she lifted off, she said, "I am a princess on my world. Maybe some time in the future you come to my world and will keep me company for awhile?"

I chuckled. "Thank you for the offer, my lady, but you'd tire of me very quickly. There is more to a relationship than just sex. Besides, they wouldn't even let me into your palace. I'm a *Nobody*."

"I can't believe that. You travel in the company of two *Outsiders*, so you must be very important."

"Outsiders? Are you talking about my companions?"

"They are from outside explored space. Surely you know."

"I know nothing about them. How do you know of them?"

She didn't smile when she answered. "A ship landed on our planet some time ago. It was of unknown design. The people it carried used devices to communicate with us. They didn't speak the common language. They told us they had come a long way in search of artifacts. Your companions were among the crew. Now they are with you. Who are you?"

I shrugged. "I told you, I am nobody. My name is Thomas Reginald Stone. I used to be a commodore with the Terran Space Force."

"Used to be? Explain!"

I gave a short laugh. It sounded like a dog barking. "It's a boring, sad story. Believe me, you don't want to hear it." I put my hand behind her furry neck, pulled her down and kissed her...hard. She didn't respond, pulled away when I let her go. Shrugging her slim shoulders, she sat up.

I turned to look at the other female.

"Let me see your face," I said.

She shook her head. "I am a servant. Nobody is allowed to see my face."

"You don't want to see her face," the princess said. "It will haunt you forever."

"That's a long time." I smiled, looking at the beautiful, alien face of the princess. "I guess one face to haunt my dreams is enough."

"Mine?" she asked and laughed.

"And your voice," I said. "When you talk it sounds like a song."

"Then you should come to my planet. You will never get tired listening to our females talk." She laughed again. "Our males think that we talk too much. They don't listen anymore."

"Those two males with you, are they your mates?"

"No. One is my brother, the other one a cousin." She cocked her head, listened to the cries of pleasure coming from the next room. "Your *Outsider* companions seem to match our male's sexual prowess." She turned suddenly and raked her long fingers across my naked chest. Her nails were sharp and drew red lines into my skin.

I watched the tiny droplets of blood appear, like rows of red spheres.

She bent over me, let her head drop into my lap. Her mouth opened, sucked in my limp penis. Even though I felt tired, I reacted immediately to the unexpected stimulus. Her satiny tongue flicked over the swollen head, and then sharp teeth sank into the shaft, making me cry out with the sudden pain.

Her face looked vicious, her eyes cold.

"Thomas Reginald Stone," she said, "you will remember the pleasure I gave you, but remember this also, had I chosen to I could have inflected terrible pain. I am capable of it."

I stared at her. "Where I come from we call women like you bitches," I murmured in the Terran tongue. Then I reached for her, pulled her close. She struggled, but I threw her onto her back, climbed on top of her. With one hand I forced open her thighs, spread them with the weight of my body. Her fists pummeled my chest, but I ignored her. Pushing hard I entered her moist, hot orifice.

I don't rape women, but I knew this is what she wanted, and

needed.

Gasping, she pushed up against me, taking me deep inside her. Her body shook in the grip of an orgasm and her juices were flowing freely. I didn't wait too long before I came inside her. She cried out sharply in her native tongue, when she felt my discharge. My own voice sounded harsh in my own ears.

I stayed inside her when I was finished, wondering if she wanted to go on, but she sighed deeply and gave me a gentle stab between my ribs.

"You are an extra-ordinary being," she said, still breathing hard.

I knelt beside her, cupped one of her soft purple breasts. "So are you, Your Highness," I said.

She smiled lazily, put one of her long fingers on my nose, then my lips. "You must visit me some day, Thomas Stone."

Then with a fluid motion, she rose to her feet, stood naked above me. I drank in the sight of her, her tall, slim form, her shapely long legs, her perfectly formed up-tilted breasts, and her exquisite face. In the shaded light that fell through the window the purple fuzz that covered her body seemed to glow softly.

"You are a beautiful woman," I said, and meant it.

She laughed that strange laugh of hers and placed a foot on my chest; slowly she trailed it down my belly and let it come to rest in my groin. Below her belly, the white hairless muscles that framed her sex-organ rippled smoothly. Her long toes curled around my penis, began stroking it. When I reacted she smiled and took away her foot. Then she turned, presenting her round buttocks and her curved back. Her dark purple hair was streaked with white, long on top, the part that grew out of her spine trimmed short.

She said something to the servant-girl, who brought a small cloth and began rubbing down her soft fur. She twisted her slender body slowly under the servant-girl's brushing hands, pushed back her buttocks, arched her back and thrust out her breasts.

She knew that I watched her. Once in awhile she threw glances in my direction and smiled.

I closed my eyes and listened to the sounds coming from the front room, picturing Sharina and Kabrina writhing in ecstasy underneath those two males. I listened to their ecstatic cries with mixed feelings. Should I be jealous? Was I jealous? I didn't know.

So much for their declaration of their love for me. Of course, they had never promised to be faithful.

While I lay there naked, I suddenly wondered why I didn't feel cold. Opening my eyes, I looked around and saw the little atomic heater standing in the corner.

Another expensive piece of technology.

The princess saw my look and smiled. "We like to travel in comfort," she said. "These backwards planets can be so primitive."

She began to put on her skintight outfit. Dressed, she walked out of the room.

The masked servant-girl closed the door behind her, and then she came back and knelt beside me. Her soft, long fingers touched my chest, then slid down my stomach, came to rest on my penis. Gently, she wrapped her fingers around it; massaging it slowly, she brought me to a full erection. Then she bent over me and began to perform fellatio. My hard penis strained inside her hot mouth. When I thought I couldn't stand it any longer she freed me, turned and slipped her creamy, hot sex-organ over my shaft, like a tight, well-fitting sheath.

She presented her back to me. I watched her move above me with a steady rhythm. Her plump white buttocks flattened when they touched my belly, but returned to their flawless shape when she lifted up. Between them I got glimpses of my penis. It disappeared again as she sank down, taking it back into her belly.

I reached around her, cupped her soft breasts, and then I pulled her backwards. She was very supple, and kept snapping her hips up and down. There seemed to be no bone inside her the way she moved her lower body.

She tightened her inner muscles, squeezed tightly. I felt the hot fluid of her discharge as she climaxed. Without uncoupling I rolled us over, ending up on top of her. Snapping my pelvis, I rammed my hard member between her soft buttocks. She kept on milking and pushed her clenching buttocks up into my groin.

She pushed up. I yielded, moved with her until she was on her knees. Kneeling behind her, I moved in and out of her hot, tight sheath, my hands still holding onto her breasts.

"Now!" She called out suddenly and quivered in my grasp. I was ready. With a deep cry I spilled my seed into her, felt it gushing out of me, just to be sucked up by her clutching sex-organ.

It seemed to go on forever.

Then it ended. Her soft cries of pleasure stopped. She stayed in that kneeling position for a long time. Still inside her, I buried my face in the thick purple hair growing out of her spine.

She sighed, and then she said softly, "Never before has any male made me feel this way. I could go on for a long time yet, but we must stop now."

I chuckled into her hair. "I think you've sucked the last drop out of me. I am exhausted." I pulled out of her, with much regret, but stayed on my knees as she straightened her body. Turning around, she faced me.

"I am going against tradition now," she said and pulled the mask from her face.

My eyes must have betrayed me, because she laughed gently and touched my face. "You don't like what you see?" she asked.

I didn't answer, just stared.

The alien beauty of her face seemed almost unreal, and when she smiled, it lit up the room.

I only saw her perfectly shaped face, her lips, her nose, her purple eyes. Nothing else existed at the moment.

"It is no surprise that you are not allowed to show your face in the presence of the princess. She is very beautiful, but your beauty outshines hers tenfold." I spoke those words, and I was in love.

I had seen and loved many beautiful women, not one of them like this servant-girl.

She put her lips on mine, kissed me gently. Her mouth opened, her tongue met mine. She tasted exotic, sweet, like a heady aphrodisiac. It made my head spin.

We broke apart, gasping for breath.

She put her mask back over her face. The sun seemed to disappear behind thick clouds.

"Maybe it was a mistake," she whispered.

I shook my head. "No. It would have been a mistake to deny me such beauty. I will always remember you. The princess was right. You will haunt my dreams forever."

Chapter Eight

As promised, the Flemlins lent us their anti-gravity belts. The servant-female accompanied us. She would fly back with the three belts that we were using.

"You don't know us, yet you trust us," I said to her as she flew beside me high above the snow-covered treetops. "We could kill you and take these belts. They are worth a fortune."

She laughed softly. "You won't, you are too much in love with me."

"My companions are not."

"They felt the rods of the Prince and his cousin inside them. They are also in love."

I had to suppress a grin. Nobody would dare to rob the Flemlins. Their punishment would be swift and deadly.

It was a beautiful day. Even though the air felt cold and crisp, the sunshine made it seem warm and friendly. What would have taken us probably another two days of hellish torture, traveling over land, took us only a couple of hours by air, but when we landed I was happy to stand on solid land again.

The Flemlin female removed her mask for a fleeting moment, and the snow melted around me. How could anyone be so beautiful? She gave me a kiss on the lips, smiled and looked into my eyes. "Take care, Thomas Reginald Stone." Then she whispered into my ear, "Beware your companions, they are *Outsiders*."

She adjusted her facemask, put the three anti-gravity belts into a small backpack and shot into the air. She'd be back in the cabin before dark.

I looked around. We landed in the middle of a small fishing village. I counted no more than three dozen houses from the air. A blanket of deep snow covered the road that led through the village. Only vehicles on air cushions would be able to travel on this road.

The village lay on the shore of a frozen lake. The strong wind blew the snow off the ice, and the rays of the setting sun painted the glinting ice red. I saw a pair of fishermen pulling small sleds behind them, on their way back to shore. Everything looked very peaceful.

Sharina and Kabrina had disappeared into one of the buildings. A sign above the door proclaimed it a tavern. Who would have guessed?

The only tall building in this forsaken place, and the drunk falling out of the door should have been a dead giveaway.

There were two air-sleds parked in the small parking lot, they held no markings, but they gave me the shivers. These were no ordinary air-sleds.

I followed the girls into the tavern.

The place didn't look crowded, no surprise, considering the size of the village. The surprise came with the man sitting at one of the tables. He didn't wear a uniform. However, the man with him did. I recognized the uniform and the insignia on the man's left sleeve. A high-ranking officer in the *United Planet's Space Navy*.

I approached the table slowly.

"Hello, Thomas, good to see you again."

"Admiral," I said, but I didn't salute.

He smiled. "We had a hard time tracking you down, son," he said.

"Had I known you wanted my company, I would have left you a note, Father," I said. No, I was not bitter.

He sighed. "I can't blame you if you hate me." He indicated the empty chair across from him. "Sit down."

I shrugged and sat down.

"This is Colonel Voltaire," Admiral Curtis said.

The Colonel gave me a courteous nod. "Pleased to meet you, Commodore Stone. I've heard a lot about you."

"I'm sure you have. You can drop the 'Commodore'. I'm just plain 'Thomas Stone'. I don't believe they missed to mention that small detail when you were briefed about me."

Colonel Voltaire smiled thinly. "I am aware of your situation, Commodore. I know that you have been discharged without honor from the Service. I also know that there are people out there who want you dead. You are the victim of a conspiracy, Commodore, but you know that already."

He possessed hard eyes, this colonel, they showed no pity, but they were honest.

"You didn't come here to tell me that you feel sorry for the way I was treated, Colonel. What do you want from me?" I glanced at Admiral Curtis, but his face remained passive.

The Colonel laughed. "Coming right to the matter, Commodore. I like that."

"It's been a long day and I am very tired." I said. "I need a meal, a bath and a good night's rest."

"We have made arrangements for a room where you can sleep safely. You won't have to fear for your life tonight, you'll be well guarded."

My turn to laugh. "Are you afraid I'm going to escape?" I asked. I had seen the two *Colonial Marines* at one table and the two *Special Troopers* at another.

"You are not a prisoner, Thomas." Admiral Curtis said. "By the way, your mother sends her regards. She misses you."

"I miss her too," I said, speaking the truth, especially since we hadn't seen much of each other for the last two years.

"You shouldn't have left." The Admiral said softly. I always thought of him as just *The Admiral,* even though he was my stepfather. We had been close, or so I thought. After I was court-martialed, he buried himself in his work, refused to see me when I attempted to contact him.

"I feared for my life," I said. "They murdered everyone else. Why not me, why was I humiliated like that?"

He stared at me. I saw the pain in his eyes. "Because you are my son, that's why. I am not very popular with certain people, but I am in a position of power; they cannot get rid of me that easily. You were the more convenient target."

"That may be true, but there is more to it, isn't there?"

He nodded. "You carry dangerous knowledge inside your head."

"Like what?"

"The co-ordinates to an unknown planetary system."

"I was told that I made all that up."

Admiral Curtis looked at me gravely. "That's what they want everyone to believe; that is why you had to be discredited. I went through old, forgotten files in the archives from the early colonization programs. What I was mostly interested in were reports about lost colony ships, and I did find one intriguing entry. This file is about a thousand years old. Apparently, one of the colony ships dropped out of subspace before it reached its final destination. The onboard computer sent a message back to Earth reporting the failure of the warp-drive. There was a suitable planet close-by, and if the drive could not be repaired, the colonists would be brought out of stasis and transported down to the planet. Unfortunately, the computer was not programmed to configure the co-ordinates of the system."

"Interesting," I said, "but there is no proof that it is the same system I dropped into, is there?"

Admiral Curtis smiled. "The report mentions black delta-shaped spaceships."

I listened only half-heartedly to his story. I was tired and my skin started to itch inside the outdoor suit I wore, but this got my attention. "Who else knows about this?" I asked.

"I've told only Colonel Voltaire."

"Why him?"

"We've been friends for a long time, even though he is a Colonial. Our paths have crossed many times. I know I can trust him, and he knows more about lost colonies than anyone else does. Besides, I needed him to find you. After all, Korillia is not part of the Terran Empire."

Before I could query him, a familiar voice interrupted us. "Why don't you let poor Thomas get some rest before he collapses?"

I looked at Sharina who came up behind Colonel Voltaire. She already removed her outerwear, and now she was dressed in black, loose-fitting pants and shirt. Even though her sister Kabrina wore the identical outfit, I recognized Sharina who spoke. There were subtle differences between them after all, and I learned to tell them apart. She bent closer to the colonel and said, "Thanks for the supplies."

It didn't take a genius to figure out that they knew each other. The gun she now strapped to her narrow waist hadn't been there before.

"Am I correct to assume that you and your sister are not just a couple of prostitutes hired to entertain me?" Sometimes I say things I shouldn't, but seeing her so close to Voltaire made me irritable.

She pouted. "After all we've been through, you say such terrible things?"

I shrugged, stared at Voltaire. "Who are these two?" I asked him.

The colonel smiled. "The best two agents I ever had. They are not human, you know. They may look human, but they're not."

"I would have never guessed." The sarcasm was not lost on him, but he ignored my remark.

"They've been in our Service for only a year, but they have proved loyal, and they are a great asset to my department." Colonel Voltaire touched Sharina on her hip with a familiarity I resented.

"You're fucking them?" I asked bluntly. "They're good at that."

He never lost his smile, but his eyes grew hard. He removed his hand from Sharina's hip. "I think you should get some rest," he said.

"Hopefully, you'll be more amiable in the morning."

Admiral Curtis gave me a long look, and then he sighed. "I apologize for my son's behavior," he said to the colonel. "He is a good man and usually quite civilized."

"For someone who was nothing but a filthy savage only 15 years ago," I chuckled.

The colonel cocked an eyebrow. "Meaning what?"

"Nothing." Admiral Curtis looked at me, shook his head. "Get some sleep, Thomas. We'll talk in the morning."

Chapter Nine

The girls didn't share my room, and I was glad for the privacy. It had been quite a day, or more precisely, quite a week. I haven't had this much sex in years. Actually, I've never had this much sex. I made it my policy not to fraternize with the women in my outfit, and I spent the last two years mostly in space, chasing pirates.

I must have fallen asleep immediately, but sleep was not restful.

* * * *

He waited for me in my dreams, mocking me with his laughter. His golden body shimmered in the bright sun as he rose into the sky on giant wings. I followed him, warm air caressed my naked skin as I slid through the energy currents that eddied around the planet below.

"You cannot follow me!" I heard his voice inside my head. Bolts of lightening shot from his fingers, but I absorbed the energy, used it to feed my own needs. An army of black winged creatures surrounded him. Their bodies blocked the bolts of energy I threw at him.

Suddenly I felt drained. Losing my powers, I tumbled out of the sky toward the planet's surface.

* * * *

I woke up, drenched in sweat, the dream still real.

Who was that winged man? What did this dream mean?

It still looked dark outside, but I couldn't sleep anymore, so I lay there, contemplating my life and assessing the situation. Only a few months ago my life had been orderly. I had a purpose. I had friends. Now they were all gone, and here I was, hiding like a rat from an unseen enemy who wanted me dead. Why? What was so important in that stellar system that even knowing its location proved dangerous?

Whoever resided on that planet possessed far advanced technology. So why were these people hiding? What were they afraid of? Obviously, they had spies in the Terran Empire, spies who held connections to influential and important officials. Enough influence to have people killed, or discredited. Those Thorans, who had come to assassinate me, somebody had hired them. Who?

My dream still haunted me. That golden, winged man, he looked familiar. I made a sudden connection to a new religious cult that attracted followers throughout the known Galaxy. They worshipped a god they called *The Golden Lightbringer*, an all-powerful immortal being who would unite and lead the Galaxy to eternal glory. The time of his appearance was close. They called themselves the *Galactics.*

Cults come and go, but this one was the latest one, its members were becoming a nuisance on many planets, and some governments were beginning to persecute them.

Nobody had any proof, but there were rumors that the Galactics were responsible for a number of assassinations.

When the humans began to explore the Galaxy, they found other inhabited planets. Some developed space-travel, some had not. Like Earth, all planets maintained their own religions, many similar to what humans believed. All believed in good and evil forces, forgiving gods and vengeful gods. Many believed in super-beings who once ruled the Galaxy. Immortal super-beings. After reaching a certain stage in their evolution, they disappeared. Nobody knew what happened to them, but the common belief was that they left watchers behind who guarded the Galaxy. These Immortals lived on many planets, undetected, unknown, and only when needed did they reveal themselves.

The cult of the Galactics sprang out of these legends.

I never even expressed an interest in these people, so why then would they be after me?

I must have dozed off, because a knock on the door made me open one eye. Daylight filtered through the shutters of the window. "Come in," I called, rubbing the sleep from my eyes.

Sharina stepped into the room. She looked rested and as beautiful as ever, her long hair loosely tied with a purple ribbon to keep it from falling into her face. The black, loose-fitting outfit she wore didn't hide the swell of her hips and breasts. The only thing I didn't like was the gun she now strapped to her waist. It looked small and almost harmless, but its size didn't fool me.

Walking over to the window, she pulled up the shutters to let the light stream in.

"Everybody is waiting for you, Thomas," she said brightly.

"Go away," I said and pulled the covers over my face. I hated that bright sunshine when I felt so gloomy.

Laughing, she grabbed the sheet and pulled it away from my body, leaving me exposed. I don't wear pajamas, never mind the fact that I didn't have any.

She threw herself onto the bed beside me. Her hand encircled my semi-erect penis. "We can let them wait a little while longer," she murmured into my ear.

My member grew under her touch. I didn't feel like having sex right now, but I needed to vent my anger, and I didn't struggle when she pinned me down. Straddling me, she took off her belt and pulled the shirt over her head. I watched her large breasts tumble free. Then she pushed down her pants, slid them past her hips exposing her hairless pubis. Very slowly she pulled first one leg out of the pant-leg, and then the other. Naked, she lifted up, and in slow motion she fed my stiff pole into her.

Her strange emerald eyes locked with mine, her lips pulled into a half-smile. She shook loose her long hair, letting it spill onto her shoulders. Gently, she rippled her inner muscles along my shaft, and then she began to rotate her hips.

I reached up, pulled her down, crushed her breasts against my chest, then I rolled her onto her back and rammed myself deep into her.

"Easy, Thomas!" she cried out, but I didn't feel like being gentle and fucked her hard. She screamed and raked my back with long, sharp fingernails, but she didn't experience any pain. Her juices were flowing freely, and when I came inside her, she dug her heels into my buttocks and milked my spurting member furiously.

Spent and feeling much better I lay panting beside her. She laughed softly and got up to go to the bathroom.

It felt like deja-vu, but when I opened my eyes to look around the room, it didn't take long to get back to reality.

I hadn't heard the door open, but when I saw the figure of someone standing in the doorway I almost expected to see Kabrina, but it wasn't, just one of the Colonial Marines. Why do Security-Men never smile? They must be a special breed.

"Is everything alright in here?" he asked, his eyes scanning the room.

"Why shouldn't it be?" I asked.

"I thought I heard screams," he said.

Sharina padded back into the room, wearing nothing but a sweet smile. Even a cold-blooded fish like this marine couldn't hide his emotions that well. His eyes widened for a moment and a tick moved his upper lip.

"Relax," Sharina smiled at him. "Tell Colonel Voltaire we'll be there shortly."

"Yes, sir." The marine backed out of the door, closed it behind him.

Sharina laughed, stood wide-legged in front of me. "Are you still angry?" she asked.

"Why would I be angry," I said, letting my eyes travel over her body. Damn, she looked beautiful. How could I be mad at her?

She touched my cheek. "I told you I love you, Thomas. So does Kabrina."

I sighed and sat up. "Cut the crap, Sharina. I am a job to you, that's all. You're not even human, how do I know what the concept *Love* really means to you."

She pouted and began to dress. "The same as it does to you," she said in a low voice when she was dressed. Her eyes glowed softly when she looked at me, but I couldn't read anything in them.

* * * *

The Admiral and Colonel Voltaire sat at one of the tables. I smelled bacon and eggs.

"Feeling better?" My stepfather asked as I planted myself into a chair beside him.

"Much," I said, giving him a tight smile. "But I'm sure it'll go away."

Admiral Curtis shook his head. "This isn't like you, Thomas. And, please, don't take your anger out on me. I know, you think you have a right to be angry with me, and maybe you do. If I had any sense I would just forget this whole thing and leave you to your fate."

"So what's stopping you?"

He looked at me, his eyes hurting. "If you must ask...," he said softly.

"I'm sorry." I looked at his plate, smiled. "Looks like eggs and bacon, but what is it?"

It was the colonel who chuckled. "Sometimes it is better not to know."

I shrugged. "Not always. But what the hell, I'll have some of that."

I barely finished saying it when a waitress approached our table, carrying a tray. She sat it down in front of me. "Wow!" I said. "Sunny side up, just the way I like it."

The girl smiled at me, but didn't say anything.

"I took the liberty to order for you," the Admiral said.

I felt ravenous and grateful when they let me eat my breakfast without conversation. I knew they were watching me, but I didn't let it bother me. When I was finished I wiped my mouth with a serviette that would have been more suitable as a floor-mat, leaned back in my chair and said, "So, what is it you want from me?"

Admiral Curtis leaned forward, looked me straight in the eyes. "We want you to go to that unknown system and find out who these people are?"

"Just like that!" I couldn't help but laugh. "You're serious?"

"Totally." His eyes never left my face. "We have to know who we are dealing with. It is obvious, they have spies among us, and we know nothing about them. You are the only one I can trust."

"Last time I dropped in on these people I was not exactly welcomed with open arms. You read my report."

He nodded. "I did."

"How do you expect me to sneak up on them?"

"You won't have to. We figure they'll let you land without any problems, after you explain who you are." His lips twitched a little. I knew him well enough to know that he was having fun.

"Don't keep me in suspense. Who will I pretend to be?"

"A pirate."

"A pirate?"

"That's right, a pirate." He grinned. "After you got kicked off the force you were so angry that you wanted nothing but revenge. What better is there but turning to piracy. Don't you think it is a good plan?"

"It stinks. How the hell can I become a pirate? I can't just flag down the next pirate-ship that comes along and ask them if they have room for another pirate. Come one, I expected a better plan."

"That's where Colonel Voltaire comes in. He does have connections with certain elements, as a matter of fact, he's already been in contact with an old friend of his and made some arrangements."

The colonel cleared his throat. "I wouldn't call him an old friend; he's more or less just an acquaintance. I don't want Commodore Stone to get the wrong impression."

I looked at him. "Does it really matter what I think of you?" I asked him.

He didn't smile. "Not really, but I want you to trust me. It does make for a better relationship. Besides, two of my agents will accompany you. If you don't trust me, how can you trust them?"

"Those two agents, I assume you're talking about Sharina and

Kabrina?"

He nodded. "That is correct. They'll be a definite asset to you." His expression seemed cool, but his eyes were not too steady when he said that.

I admit: I wasn't exactly disappointed. They could have teamed me up with a couple of ugly, old crones. "What's in it for me?" I asked.

"I don't want to deceive you, Thomas," Admiral Curtis said slowly. "And I can't make any promises. This is not an official mission. You are strictly on your own. We'll see."

"Not much of an incentive, is there? Maybe I'll like being a pirate."

I watched the waitress clean the table. She was Korillian, humanoid, and not hard to look at, if you overlooked the bulging eyes and the flat nose. She did have full, round buttocks with a nice wiggle to them when she walked. I wondered how she behaved in the sack.

"How did you ever come up with this idea that I should masquerade as a pirate?" I asked, still watching the girl as she lithely moved between the tables.

The Admiral sighed, and I looked at him. He knew the whole thing didn't excite me very much. "The pirate-ship you chased disappeared into the atmosphere of that mysterious planet…unchallenged. That means it was not unexpected, it obviously had business there," he answered.

"It could also mean that it was one of theirs," I said. "I'll be a total stranger. What if they decide to blow me into tiny atoms before I have the chance to explain who I am?"

"There is that chance," he said gravely. "Nobody forces you to go through with this. I will not stop you if you get up now, tell us to get lost and take that girl you've been watching up to your room and fuck your brains out. It is your choice, but I know you'll do the right thing."

"I could accept your offer and still do that." I grinned. He knew me better than anyone else; couldn't fool the old fox.

"This is serious business, Thomas. I wish we could find another way. You may think whatever you want about me, but, damn it, you are my son. I love you like my own flesh and blood. I would never willingly send you to certain death. This is your chance to exonerate yourself."

This sudden outburst took me a little by surprise. I've never seen him this emotional. "I'll do it," I said softly. "What do I have to lose?" I smiled at him. "Besides, I'm not really that busy at the moment."

"No, you're not." He returned my smile. "Colonel Voltaire will give you the details."

Chapter Ten

"Sometimes I wish I could hide in a place like this." Admiral Curtis stopped walking, stood for a moment to catch his breath. "Getting old." He smiled. "Maybe I'm just out of shape. Too much time spent behind a desk."

"The air is cold," I said. "You're probably not used to it." A few large snowflakes were beginning to fall, but I didn't think it would lead to anything we'd have to worry about. We had plenty of snow already on the ground. A couple more centimeters wouldn't matter.

"I never really cared much for snow." The Admiral looked across the frozen lake. "I was stranded once for weeks on a planet that was mostly frozen tundra. The planet was hostile and so were the inhabitants." Blowing into his hands, he rubbed them together vigorously. "Your mother doesn't mind the snow," he said. "And I know you don't, either."

"It doesn't bother me much," I said. I knew he was just making small-talk. Something was troubling him.

"Listen," he said suddenly, "I am sorry about what happened after you were court-martialed. Maybe I should have shown more support; you certainly needed it. But there are forces at work here that scare the hell out of me. I don't know anymore whom I can trust. That was another reason I contacted Colonel Voltaire."

I turned my head to look at the two Marines who were following us at a short distance. The big *Mark Sevens* they carried casually and their watchful eyes didn't comfort me as much as they should have. "Are you in any danger?" I asked.

He shrugged. "If I were assassinated it would certainly spawn an investigation by the Imperial Council, but who knows how deep the government and military have been infiltrated."

"Infiltrated?"

"Just a figure of speech." He looked around as if anyone could overhear his accusation. "There are many people I don't trust. Admiral Sasmussen is one of them."

"Why not confront him?"

"He is highly connected. His brother-in-law sits on the Imperial Council."

"Politics!" I bent down and scooped up a handful of snow, wet and easily molded into a ball. I threw it as far as I could, watched it disappear in the small snow bank I aimed for. The Admiral chuckled and bent to make his own snowball, threw it. It fell short of its intended target.

"I've never been good at throwing a ball," he said. I remembered the few times we played baseball together and had to agree. He touched my arm, looked at me. "I've never told you this, Thomas, but when I met your mother and consequently you, I did have you investigated. I was curious about your past. I didn't find out anything about you. It seems you never existed before your mother found you on that planet. But I did discover something. Did you know that an ancestor of yours was a colonel with the Space Force a hundred years ago?"

I stopped abruptly, turned to stare at him. "How did you find that out?"

"Purely by chance, actually. I was studying the short war the Terran Empire fought with an insectoid race on Sirius V. One of the people responsible for winning that war was a Colonel Roger Davis. The resemblance to you is uncanny. You could be his twin. Of course, I have no proof he was a blood relation. He wasn't married, seemed to have no immediate family, and didn't leave a trail I could follow. If he is an ancestor he obviously did father at least one child. Apparently, he was killed a few years after the war in a freak accident. No details available, either."

"Why didn't you tell me this?"

"I felt guilty for investigating you. It could have been interpreted the wrong way." His smile seemed forced. "I'm a suspicious person by nature, and your assumption would have been correct. I didn't trust you."

"You trust me now?"

"Truth?" He looked at with grave eyes. "You're still an enigma to me, but, yes, I trust you. With my life, if necessary. You are my son!" He took me by surprise when he hugged me. I don't mind hugging, as long as it's a woman I hug. Men hugging has always struck me as a little creepy. "Sorry." He smiled when he let me go. "I know you're not the huggable type."

"Neither are you."

He walked on, pulled the collar of his coat tighter around his neck. The wind shifted direction, it started blowing into our faces, and the snow was still coming down.

"Snowflakes," he said, "so fragile and such a short lifespan. Lately I've become more aware of my own mortality. I've had a long life, long by human standards, but less than the blink of an eye in the existence of the universe. Will anyone even remember me when I'm gone? What will my legacy be?"

"Are you trying to tell me something?" I asked.

"Like what?"

I shrugged. "Did you contract some kind of incurable disease? Are you dying?"

"No, nothing like that." He laughed. "I hope to be around for a long time still. Your mother and I had a discussion the other day. She's obsessed with finding evidence that the legendary race of the *Guardians* actually existed. If they ever did, nobody seems to remember them."

"The Galactics believe in them."

"The Galactics!" He snorted with disgust. "They also believe in the winged Golden God. They're a bunch of dangerous fanatics."

"I have to agree with you there. Come let's turn back. My face is getting cold."

He clasped my shoulder. "You don't have to do this, you know. No one's forcing you. Obviously, you'll be putting yourself in harm's way, but I can't think of anyone else who'd have a chance to succeed. You and your team were the best we had. Too bad about the others."

"Yes, too bad. They were good men. Nobody questioned their deaths."

"I did. But my hands were tied…still are. But it isn't over yet, I promise you that."

"Colonel Voltaire! How well do you actually know him?"

"Well enough. That ice-planet I mentioned: it was the Colonel who found and rescued my men and me. He could have left us there, but he put himself and his ship in danger to get us out."

"You never told me that story."

"It happened a long time ago, long before I married your mother." Admiral Curtis looked at the barely visible buildings of the little town. The snow had been falling quite heavy for the last ten minutes. The two Marines were walking on either side of us now. They didn't seem to be bothered by the snow. "He is a good man. A good soldier with honor. You can trust him."

Chapter Eleven

Tagnaroc. The city sprung up around the spaceport. Not as large as Caldrak, the main spaceport on Korillia, but big enough to get lost in…if you wanted to. Most of the space shuttles that docked in Tagnaroc carried illegal contraband and passengers who tried to avoid the regular ports. That did not mean that the people who lived in Tagnaroc were all crooks and thieves, but looking around in the tavern we were in, one could certainly get that impression.

"Well, where is this contact we are supposed to meet?" I asked the girls.

Sharina shrugged. "He'll be here. Just relax, Thomas."

I was watching Kabrina who struck up a conversation with some guy at the bar. I didn't care much for the way his hand stroked her buttocks and the way she acted as if she didn't notice it. "Your sister is getting pretty friendly with that guy," I commented.

Sharina laughed and touched my nose with her finger. "Jealous, Thomas?" she asked.

"Not jealous, just cautious. I don't want to attract too much attention." I lied. Of course I was jealous.

"You blend in just fine. Nobody cares about you here." She was right about the blending in. I wore a pair of tight-fitting black pants, a black shirt and a loose black coat that went down to my knees. Thick-soled black high boots finished the outfit.

Oh, I forgot about the black skullcap.

Sharina and Kabrina were dressed the same way, except that their coats barely covered their tight little asses. It seemed to be the dress code around here, because most patrons were dressed in similar fashion. Except for the waitresses. They wore next to nothing. I never knew that the Korillians had two navels.

The majority of patrons were human, or humanoid, but I also saw a bunch of Vegans, impossible to miss their saurian faces, not to mention their rude and loud behavior.

At the table beside us sat two Kapellans, birdlike beings with long, thin necks. They looked like a couple of harmless travelers, until you saw the huge guns strapped to their narrow waists. Apparently, their species possessed ill tampers. I had no intention of finding out.

Kabrina finished the drink she had been nursing and started

walking toward our table, her new acquaintance in tow. "This is Tortes," she introduced him and pulled a chair over from another table.

Tortes bowed and looked at me. I noticed his artificial eye and knew that it transmitted my image onto somebody's computer-screen, where it would be analyzed and verified. I hoped that Colonel Voltaire did a thorough job.

"I am Thomas Stone," I said.

He grinned. "I know who you are, Commodore Stone."

"Then you have the advantage, Torkes," I said.

"Actually it is *Lieutenant* Torkes, in the service of the *Red Hawk Planetary System.*"

"I see." I gave him my best smile. He was our man. The Red Hawk Planetary System was a solar system without planets. Millions of asteroids circled the G-type Primary, and pirates occupied the largest ones, dangerous territory to navigate, and a perfect place for criminal elements.

"I'm told you are looking for a sponsor," Torkes said. The Red Hawk pirates were like a Union, they were quite possessive about their trade, and they hated competition. Anyone getting involved in piracy and not flying the Red Hawk flag was quickly eliminated.

"You heard correctly. I need a sponsor, and I need protection," I told him.

He gave me a long, searching look. "If it's just revenge you're seeking you don't need to join the Brotherhood," he said slowly.

"Not just revenge. I have other motives and interests, and they might just be of interest to the Brotherhood."

"Like what?"

"I know of an unknown system that harbors *Trades-people.*"

"There have been reports of other *Trader-ships,*" he mused. "What do you know of them?"

Well, I had his interest. "Not much, but I want to find them."

"Why?"

"That is my business," I smiled. "Let's say, they owe me."

"Revenge, again, but as you say, that is your business. What do you want from us?" he asked.

"I need a fast ship and, as I mentioned, protection. Money is no problem. I have resources."

"Protection is expensive. We want more than just money."

"I am aware of that, and that is not a problem, either." Hell, it wasn't! It involved having one of their surgeons implant a tiny chip into my skull, which could be used to take my head clean off my shoulders. It had other uses, too. Once a brother, always a brother!

Lieutenant Torges shrugged. "I have a shuttle waiting."

We lifted off within the hour. There were no formalities in this spaceport. A few greased palms and the officials looked the other way when it came to clearing our IDs. Most of the IDs that visitors to this place used, were fakes anyway, so it didn't matter.

The ship we docked with looked like a freighter. It carried the name *Red-Hawk-Trading-Consortium* on its belly. However, no freighter ever did get outfitted with such heavy armament, and once inside it I had no doubts about the real identity of this vessel. Too much space dedicated to carry personnel. Men and women who were armed to their teeth.

The lieutenant introduced me to the ship's surgeon, and before long, I had a little device inside my head that would help me to remember where my loyalties lay from now on.

Before I could make any deals of my own, I needed to go through a *training period.*

Chapter Twelve

We headed for our first destination, a system not far from Korillia. It took us a couple of days to get there. I was in one of three transport-shuttles, all of them full of heavily armed men. I wondered if they dragged me into some kind of war. Our shuttle landed beside a settlement of considerable size. The houses were plain, mainly single story buildings of simple design. The area around the settlement looked desolate. Nothing seemed to grow except for some kind of tall, purple multi-leafed plant. I recognized the plant. *Mexacline*. The bulbous roots held the hallucinogenic substance in almost pure form. A natural drug that needed very little processing. Expensive on the market and dangerous to use. Landry, the leader of our party of twelve men was a big brute with a wild beard and a bald head. He looked us over with little pig's eyes as we stepped from the shuttle.

"Hey, you," he addressed me. "You're the new guy. I'm supposed to watch you, but I don't have time for that. Behave yourself and don't get into any trouble. Carry your weapon always in sight…remember that. We are not exactly welcome here. These people are dangerous, ruthless, and rebellious. They'll kill you if you give them a chance. If in doubt, shoot first, and then talk. Understood?"

"I think so," I said. I had misgiving about this whole thing, but I had no choice except to go along, realizing from the beginning that I took part in a raid.

We were met by a group of twenty men and eight women. They blocked the road into the town. The weapons they carried might as well have been wooden clubs, compared to the weapons we brought.

"We can't give you anything this time," said one of the two men who stepped into our path.

"You don't say? Who gives you authority to speak for this town?" Landry asked him. I noticed the way he held his laser-pistol.

The man drew himself erect. "My name is William Carrel. I am the new mayor of Blacktown."

"Well, well, I am just so pleased to meet you." Landry made a mock bow. "And who are you?" He gave the other man a long stare.

"I am the new chief of police. The name's Burrows. We have decided to make a few rules here. From now on, you will pay us for what you take. No more free merchandise!"

"Listen, little man," Landry spoke coldly and without emotion, "you don't make the rules here, we do."

"What gives you the right to come here and rob us blind?" Carrel's said boldly, unable to hide the tremor in his voice. The man looked scared, but he bravely stood his ground. I knew what was coming, but found myself unable to stop it, because I couldn't afford to put myself and the mission in jeopardy.

"This!" Landry said, lifted his gun and shot the man. More shots fell, and before the people standing behind their mayor could even react, five men and two women lay dead.

"Anybody else wants to object?" Landry waved his laser-pistol, aimed it at another man. "You maybe?"

"Don't shoot, please," the man stammered. "It was Mayor Carrel's idea. We didn't really support him, but he threatened us. We had no choice but to follow him here. We will comply with your wishes."

"I think you'll have to do a little better now. We expect a healthy bonus for the problem you have caused us. As a matter of fact, next time we come, you will deliver double the quota. Is that understood?"

"Yes...sir. We will try our best," the man stammered. "Right?" He looked around for support.

"Alright then. Now...let us get busy. Go back to town and start delivering the merchandise. Go!"

They brought wagons loaded with the dried bulbs of the Mexacline-plants and sacks full of medicinal herbs. They even loaded them into the cargo-bay of the shuttle.

Our next stop was a mining town. We didn't meet any opposition there. The men and women who brought baskets filled with rare metals and gemstones looked sullen and moved with visible lethargy. They didn't speak to any of us, but I didn't miss the looks of hatred when they thought nobody was watching them. One of the women, a tall brunette with a face that once had been pretty, but now was lined and burnt from too many years of searching for gems under a sun too hot for human skin, looked into my eyes, then she spat into the gray dust. I couldn't blame her for being so hateful. She was a slave and she knew she would be one until the day she died. We left with our bounty, headed for another settlement, a place where Mexacline-roots were cultivated. When we landed at the outskirts of the town and the first deliveries were made, I noticed the absence of men. The majority of the people who brought and unloaded the wagons were women.

"What happened to the men?" I asked one of my compatriots. He just shrugged and grinned. "They thought they could cheat us," he said laconically.

When everything was stowed away inside the shuttles, Landry told us with a big grin to go and take a vacation. I had no idea what he meant, until we went into town.

"Nice to ride in style, don't you think so, friend?" The man who sat beside me in the dust-covered wagon laughed. "I can't believe how these people live here. I could never survive on a dust ball like this place. I prefer the sterile environment of a spaceship." He sneezed. "Damn dust everywhere."

The wind picked up since we landed and it blew gray dust all around us. The wagon we sat in had been built from rough boards and was not dustproof. The cruel sun started to disappear below the horizon in the east and the temperature began to drop a little. I perspired inside my uniform and could have used a bath.

We stopped in front of a building with a weathered sign above the door. *Bar and Grill*, it said. When we entered it, I noticed that there were no men. A few young women sat around on stools, and the bartender behind the counter was also a woman. Filled glasses were already waiting for us on the counter.

The bartender smiled as we walked in. "Good evening, gentlemen," she said, "I hope you have a good time tonight. My girls are ready and willing."

The man I spoke to in the wagon walked up to the bar, grabbed one of the filled glasses and downed it, then he leaned over and leered at the woman. "I think I want you tonight," he said and put his hand on her breast.

She removed his hand very gently. "I'm not available. I think you'll have a much better time with one of our younger girls."

He emptied another glass. "I like my women mature," he said. "I want you!"

The woman smiled, but it looked forced. "Somebody has to work the bar. I am the bartender, please, don't make it difficult."

I stepped up to the bar, took one of the glasses and sniffed it. It didn't smell unpleasant, so I tasted it. "This stuff isn't bad," I said to the woman behind the counter. "Do you make it here?"

"Not here," she said, "but they have a great distillery in Bannertown." She moved closer to my side of the counter and poured me another glass.

"Hey, buddy!" My comrade poked me in the ribs. "I saw her first."

I gave him a cold look and grabbed his hand. "My name isn't *buddy*, it's Thomas Stone, remember that." Then I grinned and slapped him on the back. "You don't want an old woman like her, come on. There are plenty of young pussies here who are giving you willingly what you may have to take from her. She's almost certainly all dried up, anyway."

He shrugged. "You're probably right. Maybe I should take one of the real young ones. They'll be nice and tight." He emptied another glass and walked over to one of the tables where some of the girls were watching us.

I turned back to the woman and smiled at her. "Give me another,"

She gave me a long look. She wasn't old and not even bad looking and I felt guilty about my remark, but she smiled shyly back at me.

"Thank you." She looked up when she heard the squeal of one of the girls. When I turned around, I saw my old buddy fondling one of them, he removed her top and her breasts tumbled out.

"Not here," I heard her say. "Come, let's go up to one of the rooms."

"Let's," he hollered and grabbed one of the other girls. "You too, and you." He pointed at the third one.

The girls giggled and followed him into the back. When I looked around, I noticed that most of my newfound comrades had already disappeared. I shook my head and turned back to the counter.

The woman had been watching me. "You don't seem to approve of your friend's behavior."

"They're animals," I said. "I'm not one of them."

"But you are here, with them, taking our hard-earned harvest. Because of you our men are gone, murdered, and we have to work twice as hard." She sounded bitter.

"I just joined this crowd and I don't know what has happened before. I am sorry, but I am a victim just like you." I looked into her scowling face. "Not like you, but a victim nevertheless. A victim of circumstances. Maybe some day it will all change."

She gave a short laugh. "I've lived here all my life. It has been like this since I can remember. Nothing will ever change. You can't imagine how many times I've been raped by these...these...filthy dogs. Sometimes at night, I wake up and scream. My dreams are filled with horrible nightmares. I can see the unshaven faces of my tormenters above me, feel their filthy rods inside my belly, feel them empty themselves into my womb. Do you know how many children…bastards I have carried and given life to?" She put her face into her hands and sobbed.

When I reached across the counter to comfort her, she shook off my hand. "No, please, don't touch me. You may be different from them, but you're still a man. I can't bear the touch of a man anymore."

I didn't know what to say to her, except for *I'm sorry*, but it sounded empty in my own ears.

She looked up, dried her tears with the swipe of her hand. "You better join your friends," she said. "We're being watched."

Swiveling in my chair, I saw two of the pirates looking in my direction. "Give me a bottle," I told her. She handed me a full bottle. I got up and walked toward their table. "Hey, aren't you joining in on the fun?"

"Why aren't you?"

I shrugged. "Low sex-drive, you know. Maybe next time." I put the bottle on their table. "Here, on the house, compliments of the bartender."

They both laughed, but it didn't sound friendly. "What are you? Some kind of comedian? Everything here is on the house, you idiot. Now go…get drunk and fuck some of these women. You're only doing them a favor. You may have noticed there aren't any guys around. These bitches are all horny."

"How come you two aren't part of the celebration?"

"Someone has to stay sober and guard the boys. Why do you think there aren't any men in this town?"

"I don't know. Tell me."

"Because they didn't want to play ball. They objected to our boys having some fun with their women. On one of our visits, they murdered all our men in their sleep, after they celebrated a little too much. So we had to teach them a lesson." He grinned. "I was here when we shot most of those bastards. You should have heard the wailing going on. But the women got over it. Now we have no more problems and they are eager to pleasure us."

"But you're missing out on all the fun."

He shrugged. "We'll still be here tomorrow night. This is a small vacation for us, so don't worry, I'll get my share of pussy. Maybe tomorrow you can stand guard, eh?"

"I guess, I can. Right now I'm going to have another drink and maybe I can persuade the bartender to spend some time with me." I winked at them. "You know what I mean."

I would have liked nothing better than to fry both their brains, but restrained myself. Taking the bottle with me, I walked back to the bar. "Do you have to stay behind that counter all night?" I asked her.

I saw her fear, when she stared at me. "Why?"

"I told them I'd be taking you into one of the rooms."

Her eyes grew large, her mouth twisted into an ugly mask. "I should have known better than to think you are different."

"Relax. I'm not going to rape you. But you'd be safe from anyone if you did spend the night with me. I promise, I won't touch you."

Her features smoothed out and she almost smiled. "I believe I can trust you. I hope I can. We'll go upstairs, into my own bedroom for more privacy." She took my hand, pulled me with her. I felt her hand tremble in mine and I knew she was still scared. She carried a bottle in the other hand. Her room looked simple, but clean. No fancy furniture, just a dresser with a mirror, a bed, a couch, a round table and a couple of chairs. There was a small room to one side, the door stood open and I could see a counter with a bowl and a water pitcher beside it.

"We live very primitive but comfortable enough," she said. "We could endure the hardship of this planet, if we would only be left alone." She walked into the small room and came back with two glasses and a plate with a few slices of bread on it. "Would you like to eat something? I have cheese and a bit of sausage."

"I don't want to rob you of your food," I said and sank into one of the chairs. "Another drink would be fine, though."

She smiled. "If there is one thing we have plenty of, it is food. They don't take that away from us." She put the plate on the table, went back into the little room and got a plate filled with pieces of cheese and sausage.

"Do you mind if I slip out of these clothes for awhile? It seems I have plenty of time. Might as well make myself comfortable." I stood up and took off my heavy jacket. Then I removed my gun-belt and my gun, put it beside my chair. She picked up my jacket and hung it on a hook beside the door. She looked down at my weapon, but didn't say anything.

Leaning back into the chair, I closed my eyes for a moment. Life in the military made me a hard man and immune to much of the stuff that would bother other men, but I was not heartless. I felt for these people and would have liked to help them; however I could not change anything, couldn't even protect this woman if the others wanted to do her harm.

"Why don't you eat something, it would please me." Her voice suddenly sounded soft and gentle. "I haven't taken care of a man for such a long time. I mean...prepared food for him and other domestic chores."

I opened my eyes. She removed her apron and sat on the bed. Her hair, which had been bound behind her head, hung loose down to her shoulders. "Please," she said with a low voice. "Pretend you came for a social visit."

I took a slice of bread, bit into it. It tasted fresh and a little sweet, so did the cheese, better than the synthetic stuff we usually ate on the ship. She filled the glass with a red liquid. I drank from it and discovered it was wine.

"Hmm," I said. "This is good. Dry, with no bitter aftertaste. This stuff would fetch a good price."

She shook her head. "This is reserved for our own consumptions and only for special guests. Not for sale."

"Am I to understand that I'm a special guest?"

She took a sip from her own glass, looked at me over the rim. I found her suddenly quite attractive and felt a stirring in my loins, but I suppressed it. I promised her and I wouldn't break that promise.

She drained her glass and stood up. "When I told you I can't stand the touch of a man, I didn't speak the truth," she said. "I long for a man to run his hands over my body, touch me everywhere, make sweet love to me. But it has to be on my terms."

I put down my glass. "I don't quite know how to react to that."

She grabbed the hem of her dress and lifted it up. I stared at her exposed lower body. She wore no underwear. Thick growth of black hair covered her pussy. When she pulled the dress over her head, her breasts tumbled out. They were nice and round, hardly sagging.

Throwing her dress onto the floor, she asked, "Do you know how to react to this?"

Chapter Thirteen

When I still didn't make a move, she came close to my chair and sat in my lap. "Don't tell me you're one of those men who doesn't like women?"

I inhaled her scent. It didn't help my promise to myself that I wouldn't be part of the ongoing rape of these helpless women, no matter what. She put her face against mine, flicked her tongue across my lips, then she kissed me. Her lips were warm and sweet. I tasted the liquor. Her hands moved down to my belt, began to undo it. When she slipped her hand into my pants and curled her warm fingers around my reacting penis, I groaned and kissed her back.

She laughed into my mouth and raised her body to free my straining member. Turning in my lap, she put her legs around my waist, lifted up and sheathed herself on my hard pole. She gave a little cry when I slipped into her and began to rotate her pelvis in my lap.

"For a guy who didn't seem too eager you certainly have no trouble getting into me," she groaned, her breath coming in great gasps.

"And for a woman who doesn't want anything to do with men you are much too passionate," I said, my voice somewhat hoarse from my own deep breathing. "Wouldn't it be more comfortable on the bed?"

"Much." She released me and slipped off my lap. Then she pulled me toward the bed, where she pushed me onto my back. Turning around, she presented her shapely buttocks. I grabbed her hips and pulled her into my lap, right on top of my standing pole. Wiggling her bottom, she impaled herself on my hard mast. "This feels good," she breathed and moved her lower body up and down.

After awhile she slipped off me. "Stretch out on the bed," she said. I complied and she climbed on the bed to join me. Straddling me, she hovered above me and grabbed my penis. With agonizing slowness, she descended and took me back into her hot interior. At first, she moved lazily in my lap, but after awhile she increased the tempo of her rotating pelvis. When she stopped moving and I felt her pussy walls constrict around my penis, I knew she started experiencing an orgasm. She whimpered and clawed at my hands, which I had clamped around her hips.

After she quieted down, she turned around, without uncoupling from me. Her belly rippled as she gyrated above me and her breasts jiggled deliciously. I reached up to cup them with my hands. She smiled down at me and put her hands on mine. "Squeeze them gently," she whispered.

I could feel my own climax approaching and didn't try to dampen it. "I'm coming," I shouted. She clamped down hard, almost strangled my spurting member with her tightening inner muscles.

"So am I," she cried out and sat quivering in my lap. I felt her warm juices and my own discharge running down my thighs. She sobbed and ground her buttocks into my groin until we were both spent.

But I was still hard and stayed inside her. She laughed delightedly when I pulled her down on top of me, flattening her soft breasts against my chest. I turned us both around with one mighty heave. Her legs bent sharply as she drew up her knees. Cradled by her strong thighs, I moved forcefully in and out of her.

"You are quite a man," she moaned and moved against me.

"And you're quite a woman."

She met my thrusts forcefully, her lower torso writhed beneath me with strong churning movements of her pelvis and her pussy-walls stroked my penis by squeezing it tightly every time I pushed it deep into her. When she climaxed again I released my own pressure and held her tight until she calmed down.

"I think I'm getting tired," she whispered.

We lay silent for a while on the bed. She turned suddenly and put her hand on my chest, trailed her fingers down to my belly. "Do you still think I'm some kind of dried up old woman?"

"You know I didn't mean it like that, I only said it to protect you from my so-called *friend*'s advances."

She chuckled. "I know that and I am grateful for your kindness. I knew then that you were different. What's your name?"

"Thomas," I said, "Thomas Reginald Stone."

"I am called Belicia, I was named after my grandmother." She rested her body on her elbows and looked into my face. "I let you spill your seed into me, Thomas," she said, "and it is possible that I will bear a child in nine months...your child. If that happens, I know that it was meant to be. I will not be angry and I will love that child."

"I hadn't planned to get you pregnant. I assumed you protected yourself against that kind of thing. There are many different ways to prevent pregnancies."

She chuckled. "Not here. We let nature takes its course. We need to populate our planet. Maybe some day we have enough people to stand up against marauders and others who mean to harm us. You are strong and so will your son be, perhaps he will make a difference."

She snuggled against me, her arm thrown across my chest. I closed my eyes. Suddenly I felt tired and needed a rest. Here with this strange woman I just met I felt safe.

* * * *

The gray dust swirled around us as he settled in front of me, his giant golden wings folded behind him.

"Sometimes what at first looks like a bad thing can turn into a good deed. But then again…is it?"

"You speak in riddles," I said, watching him as he picked up a handful of dust.

"Watch," he said and waved his hand; gray dust erupted from his spread fingers, enveloped us both. A strong whirlwind picked us up and swept us into the sky. The world became small, floated in space beneath a giant sun. Then we sped back to the growing sphere. Wind rushed around my body as we flew through the atmosphere toward the ground. Before we hit, I spread my wings and soared back into the sky. Floating above the world below I watched as a shuttle landed beside a city that looked familiar and yet different. I had grown in size.

Men emerged from the shuttle. They carried weapons. A small crowd of people came out of the city to greet them. The men from the shuttle demanded metals and gemstones, which the people from the city delivered to them.

I spotted a young man among the people from the city; he was large, well-built. He looked eerily familiar. There was arrogance in his walk and in the way he carried himself. "Why do we have to give all these things to these men from the sky?" he asked.

"Because we are weak and they are strong and ruthless. And because they have superior weapons."

"It is not right," said the young man.

"It is the way it has always been," answered the man to whom he spoke.

"I will make it my life's ambition to change that," swore the young man.

Darkness swirled around me, then I could see again.

The young man had gown older. He searched out others who thought like him. There were many, but most of them were afraid to stand up against the marauders.

"If we ever want to be free we have to fight them, drive them away and make sure they never come back!" He was a charismatic speaker and convinced them that they had no choice.

The shuttle landed again. After filling their shuttle with all the stuff the people brought, the marauders went into the city, as they always did, to drink and have sex with the young girls who had been chosen for that task.

When the men were drunk and sleeping, the young man and his followers cut their throats. Then they overcame the two guards who were left to guard the shuttle and took possession of it. They packed the shuttle full of explosives and told the pilot to get off their planet and to take a message back to his masters.

Again, my perception changed. I floated in space. I saw a huge spaceship circling the planet below. I recognized the name on its belly: *Red-Hawk-Trading-Consortium.*

The shuttle entered the ship. An explosion blew out part of the hull, ignited new detonations inside the ship, until one huge blast ripped apart the giant vessel.A fierce wind blew me toward the planet below. I tumbled through the atmosphere, then caught myself on my wings and glided slowly back to the surface.

"That is your legacy, the fruit of your seed." The golden man sat not far from me on a gray rock.

"Is it such a terrible thing? If this is really going to happen, will it be something evil? Does it make me evil?" I asked.

He smiled sadly. "It is never a question of good or evil. It is a question of balance. There are things that should not be meddled with." He rose. I watched him ascent into the sky on his powerful golden wings. When I tried to unfold my own wings to follow him, I discovered them gone.

Darkness reached for me from the sky. Crying out, I woke up. It took me a moment to realize where I was. Belicia stirred in her sleep. She looked so peaceful.

I touched her cheek. She smiled and opened her eyes. "Is it time to get up?" She asked.

Somebody pounded against the door to her room. "Time to leave! Finish up in there and report downstairs. On the double!"

Chapter Fourteen

Our next destination was the single moon of the fifth planet in this system. Our shuttle landed beside one of the numerous giant bubbles that dotted the ragged landscape. We taxied the shuttle through an airlock into the interior of the bubble.

There was a small town inside. The buildings were all uniform, nothing more than shacks, actually, put together from prefabricated sheets of metal.

"There will be no fraternizing with anyone here, and I'm talking about the women, understood?" Landry's pig's eyes were even smaller than usual. "This is an important source of *Quall* for us and we are not the only ones dealing with these people. So, everyone be civil!"

To my surprise I saw people coming with empty carts and actually unloading stuff from our shuttle. I helped load it onto one of their carts.

When the cart was full, the driver held out his hand. "I'm Orelli, we are sure grateful for the stuff you bring us. We wouldn't survive without it. Life here isn't exactly a picnic."

"So why do you stay here?" I asked.

He grinned. "I'm a fugitive from one of the prison-planets of the Colonies. I prefer life here to living in the hell I've escaped from. If you can imagine a place where poisonous trees grow hundreds of feet into a sky that is always purple and where animals with teeth as long as your arm, animals that are always hungry, roam the ground and the sky, then you get a tiny glimpse into the place where I spent two years...two years of absolute Hell. No, my friend, this here is Heaven."

"Are all the people here escapees?"

"Mostly the men. Our women came here freely."

I bet I thought. What sane woman would like to live under a dome all her life?

"Come, ride with me," Orelli invited me onto the seat beside him in the front of the cart. "You can help me unload and then load up the stuff we're trading."

I hopped onto the seat. We took off at a snail's pace. "These vehicles aren't exactly speedsters," Orelli said and grinned. "But beats walking."

"What precisely are you mining here?" I asked.

"Mainly *Quall*, but there are some deposits of *Cloud-crystals*, of fairly good quality. We usually get a bonus when we find them. Life isn't bad here." He glanced at me. "Probably not much different from yours. I mean, being cooped up inside a spaceship all the time?"

"I guess." He was right. There wasn't much difference. Of course, lately I had been able to visit exotic places, though not exactly by choice.

"Are you married?" I asked.

"As a matter of fact, I am." He smiled. "She's a little older than me, but a good woman. I think I lucked out when I put in my order."

"Your order?"

"We don't have an influx of women visiting us." He chuckled. "Once in while a committee takes a trip to *Shepherd's Cross*, the fourth planet, and recruits young girls or, as in my case, older women, who are looking for a husband. For some reason, there is a shortage of men on that planet. Apparently some kind of plague, I'm not sure."

Some kind of plague, indeed. I cursed inwardly. He probably knew he was dealing with pirates, but he might just be ignorant of what kind of people they actually were. Certainly not the good-hearted Samaritans they pretended to be.

We stopped in front of a larger building. There were some of the other carts already unloading their goods. "Our warehouse," Orelli explained.

We drove right inside. The place turned out to be stacked with all kinds of materials, most of the goods neatly stored on shelves. We unloaded our cart by putting everything on the floor. A small group of men and women began shelving it.

"That's my wife over there," Orelli said and pointed at an older woman. She saw him look, smiled and waved. He waved back and turned to me. "Too bad you can't stay, it would be nice to have someone over for supper and talk about other places. You must see lots of different planets. I'm sure you have plenty of stories to tell."

"Not all of them pleasant," I said. "Thanks for the invite, but I'm afraid we won't be staying for supper." I straightened my back and stretched. "More exotic and exciting places to visit, you know."

He gave me a curious glance, but said nothing. We boarded our cart again and left the warehouse. "The *Quall* is in another building," Orelli said, as we headed away from the warehouse.

The cases we loaded on our cart were much heavier than the sacks and boxes we had brought. Orelli grinned when I tried to pick up the first case by myself. "I think this job calls for two people," he said. "Quall is heavier than iron. It requires more muscles than even you have."

When we rode back to the shuttle, I looked around a little. "It would take me some time getting used to living under a transparent dome, with the stars so clear that it seems there is no air-barrier between my head and the vacuum of space." I said.

Orelli laughed. "You get used to it. We spend most of our time inside the moon anyway, digging for *Quall*."

After all the cases were stowed away in the shuttle, Orelli shook my hand again. "Nice talking to you. I never got your name."

"Stone," I said, "Thomas Stone."

"I'll remember you, Stone. I'll put in a good word for you. By the way, I'm the mayor of this dome. Actually, I'm the mayor of all the domes."

"A *Bigwheel,*" I said and grinned.

He grinned back. "Right. Nobody wanted the job, but don't tell anyone." He tipped his cap. "Maybe I'll see you next time."

* * * *

I shared a cabin with three other pirates. Two of them hardly said anything; the third one, a weasel of a man with an artificial hand, never shut up.

I had not seen the girls since we joined up with this bunch, and I wondered what they were up to. The time came to take matters into my own hands. I had no intentions to spend the rest of my days in this illustrious company. Therefore, I went to look for Lieutenant Torges.

They ran this ship like a military unit. The lowly pirates were not allowed to fraternize with the brass. We were not permitted to enter most of the areas on the ship, except for the ones designated to the lower ranks.

When I asked the sergeant in charge of our unit how I could get in touch with the lieutenant he told me I couldn't. When I insisted, he threatened to cut off my balls. I am not easily intimidated, and I take offence when someone threatens me, especially a sleaze ball like Sergeant Dimitri. After I broke his thumb and told him I would do the same with the other one, he became quite amiable and even accompanied me to the officer's quarters where he introduced me to the lieutenant's aid.

Lieutenant Torges was just having lunch with a couple of young ladies, so I was told, and it didn't surprise me when they turned out to be my long lost loving companions, Sharina and Kabrina.

"Won't you join us, Commodore," Torges invited me as I waltzed into the room.

"Don't mind," I said and sank into one of the nicely upholstered chairs. "This place is so much more comfortable than mine," I commented and accepted a glass of wine. I looked at the girls. "And how are you two? I hope you weren't too bored and lonely while I got to visit exotic places and people. Did you miss me at all?"

Sharina gave me her prettiest smile and put her hand on mine. "We've missed you so much, Thomas, but Pierro here explained to us that this was all part of the deal. Besides, he's been a good host."

"I bet he has." I eyed the lieutenant. "Well, Pierro, I think I'm ready for the next phase. Remember the small ship we've discussed?"

Torges took a deep drag from a long-stemmed pipe he was smoking and exhaled a cloud of smoke. I detected traces of *Quellin*, a mild drug that some people used for sexual stimulation. "Tomorrow we'll arrive at Arkanda. We'll be able to strike a deal there. A friend of mine has exactly what you are looking for." He grinned. "Until then, accept my hospitality. The girls and I were just about to engage in some intimate activity. Would you like to join in? I don't mind sharing."

I emptied my wineglass and stood up. "Thank you, but no. I prefer to work alone. See you tomorrow."

I didn't look back when I walked out of the door. Let them fuck each other to death, why should I care! Those two bitches didn't owe me anything, and I was not their keeper. Back in the cabin, I told the little talkative weasel to shut up before I'd make him eat his false teeth. Then I stretched out on my bunk to catch some sleep.

Lieutenant Torges kept his word. He personally took us down to the planet's surface. I could tell right away we were on another one of the pirate's strongholds.

Maybe some day I will be back with the Force, and we can clean up this little nest, I thought.

The lieutenant's friend owned a small shipyard, and he did have a ship that fit my specifications. I had no idea how the transaction would be handled, but it seemed all very professional and legal. I gave him a string of numbers, which Colonel Voltaire supplied, and the lieutenant's friend fed them into his computer.

"It may take some time," he told me. "We are a little outside the normal communication network. We'll have to go through several subspace relays."

It took more than a couple of hours until the amount we agreed upon was accepted and cleared. Torges shook my hand, winked with his good eye. "Now you can be on your way, Commodore. I will miss you. Good luck and remember to keep in touch." He touched his head and grinned. "In case you should forget we'll remind you. I think three or four months should be ample time to finish your quest."

I grinned back and nodded.

I had not forgotten that thing in my skull. To get rid of it as quickly as possible would be my priority. As if reading my mind Torges said, "Oh, by the way, in case you should develop some ideas, once it is attached to your brain it cannot be removed without removing part of your brain-matter. It is half-organic and by now has probably grown roots. Quite an ingenious device, wouldn't you agree?"

Chapter Fifteen

The ship proved quite comfortable for three people. A luxury yacht, which had once belonged to some rich, probably spoiled son of an influential family. I did not want to guess how it came into possession of my new business friends and what happened to the previous owners. The name of the ship had been erased.

We christened it *Starsurfer*.

We discovered food on board, but not enough for a lengthy journey. Neither did we have enough fuel. I checked the star-charts and found a system where we could buy what we needed. *Eden's Gate*, not a very desirable place to visit or to do business with, but the closest.

A large number of the inhabitants of *Eden's Gate* were Galactics, the cult whose members believed in the myth of the Golden Lightbringer. Could the Galactics be the ones who tried to have me assassinated? I didn't know, not even sure why I thought so. Just because I dreamed about the golden winged man, their *Messiah*, was certainly no reason to suspect them.

Nevertheless, they were responsible for assassinating people who spoke out against their beliefs. Had I unknowingly given them reason to believe I was one of those? It suddenly hit me why I had not seen the connection.

Admiral Sasmussen, the man responsible for my present predicament, he had been a member of the Galactics.

Mystery solved. Maybe. I still lacked proof.

Whatever problems I had did not change the fact that we had little choice but to go to Eden's Gate, unless we wanted to end up stranded in space. No other system happened to be close enough. We had enough fuel-crystals to make three jumps. Two jumps would get us there.

We would also be able to get cargo at Eden's Gate, a planet famous for its great variety of exotic spices, a commodity highly in demand. We did need something to trade, something that would make us welcome on the mystery planet.

Everybody loves spices.

Kabrina supervised the charging of the capacitors. It would take a few more hours until they were fully charged.

Theoretically, a bank of fully charged capacitors delivered three jumps, depending on the distance, but if things went wrong, one jump could drain the capacitors completely. No problem if the ship carried enough fuel-crystals, a disaster if it didn't. The ship would be left drifting in space. It happened.

A drifting ship provided a helpless target for raiders. I chuckled at that thought. We had the colors of the Red Hawk Planetary System painted on our hull.

"Let me in on the joke," Sharina said, looking up from the charts she studied on the small screen.

"It wasn't really funny," I said, staring at her half-exposed breasts. She saw my look and smiled. Her emerald eyes sparkled with sudden mischief.

"It'll be awhile until we're ready to jump," she said softly. "I'm getting bored. There is a big, soft bed in the stateroom, what do you say, shall we rumple it up a little?"

I did not need much encouragement, I was as horny as hell, not having had any sex for days now. Before I realized it we were out of our clothes, and I began hammering away between her clutching hot thighs.

She proved correct, the bed was large and soft, and it creaked every time I thrust into Sharina's creamy and demanding sheath.

"I missed you, Thomas," she moaned and kissed me fiercely. Then she grabbed my hips, slowed me down. "Take it easy, lover," she whispered into my ear. "We have plenty of time. Kabrina will be busy for hours."

"You don't want to share me?" I asked and dug my fingers into her solid buttocks. "Not even with your own sister?"

"Not for awhile." She cried out, pushed her hips against mine. "I need to be satisfied first. She can have you later."

We didn't speak for a long time, just moved against each other, panting and groaning. She cried out every time she experienced an orgasm, and there were several, then I couldn't hold it any longer. With a shout I burst inside her, filled her with my discharge. She held me tight, her inner muscles milking me until I was dry. Then she relaxed and kissed me tenderly.

I pulled out, lay on my back beside her, with my eyes closed, listening to her breathing as she tried to slow it down.

"You are not human," she said after awhile.

I chuckled, rolled onto my side, studied her profile as she lay there smiling with satisfaction. Reaching out, I touched her breast. It felt soft in my hand, but it was solid, strutting away from her ribcage, hardly losing its shape, even though she lay on her back.

"What do you know about humans?" I asked.

"Enough to know that you are no ordinary human male." She turned her head to look at me. Looking into her alien eyes, I remembered the Flemlin female's words.

"I was warned against you," I said softly. "You're an Outsider. You are the non-human here."

"The Flemlins!" Sharina smiled. "I've been to their planet. I am more human than they are."

"Are you? I saw you move when you killed those Thorans."

"We can move quite fast when we have to," she said. "Humans can't?"

"Not like that. Never like that!"

She sighed, turned and draped her thigh over mine. "We are different, that's all."

I looked at her smiling face. Her needle-sharp fangs gleamed dully in the soft light emitting from the walls. "Could you kill with those?" I asked.

She knew what I meant. Sliding on top of me, she pushed me onto my back and bent forward to kiss me. I felt the sharp sting in my lip, reacted immediately to the aphrodisiac. Moaning, I slipped into her moist, tight sheath. Her hips began to move lazily, her liquid vagina gripped my stiff mast powerfully.

"Only if I fuck you to death," she laughed and snapped her pelvis forward.

I let the fire race through my body, made no effort to dampen the effect of the substance she injected into me. Clamping my hands over her rotating buttocks, I pulled her tightly into my groin. Pushing deep into her, I flooded her insides with a series of powerful gushes.

She cried out sharply, stiffened in my grip. When I was finished, she went limp on top of me. "You may kill me first," she said and chuckled. "Like I said, not human."

I heard soft footsteps in the hallway as Kabrina came up from the engine-room. She pouted when she saw us naked on the bed. "That's not fair. I did all the work while you two were playing."

"He's all yours after the jump," Sharina said. "I'll let you have him."

"Oh, really! Let me tell you, sister, I will take him while you just watch."

"Hold it, girls," I said, sitting up. "I am not a commodity that can be traded back and forth. Even though I enjoy your company, this is not a pleasure trip. We have a mission."

"Oh, Thomas," Kabrina said, removing her top to expose her breasts. "You are all business. Where is the fun in that? It doesn't have to be all business." She came closer and stood in front of me as I sat on the edge of the bed. Her breasts were almost touching my face. I inhaled the fragrance her body exuded, taking a deep breath. She smelled different from a human woman, but pleasant, exciting.

Looking into my eyes, she pushed down her pants. She wore no underwear, her hairless thick vulva quivered when I put my hand on her smooth belly. Straddling me, she moved into my lap, lifted up and slipped her soft sheath over my stiff penis.

"We're not on a time schedule here, Thomas," she whispered and began to snap her pelvis back and forth. "The jump can wait, I can't." She kissed me hungrily. I hardly noticed the sharp sting in my lower lip as she bit down. I didn't really need any more of her aphrodisiac, because I was still charged up from Sharina.

After Kabrina's first orgasm I lifted her off, made her bend forward so her upper body rested on the bed, then I stepped behind her. Between her fleshy, solid buttocks her vagina-lips were thick and bulging. I put my hard member between her buttocks, slid forward and pushed deep into her greased-up sex-canal. Holding her hips, I fucked her hard and steady, slamming into her buttocks with every deep thrust.

Sharina sat cross-legged on top of the bed in front of us, watching with large eyes. Her lips were partially open, and I could hear her breathing. Then I saw her hand between her thighs, saw her hips move. I found it a tremendous turn-on and I had to fight hard to keep from coming. When it finally happened, I came with explosive force.

Kabrina squealed as I gushed inside her alien womb, pushed her buttocks backwards and up. I watched Sharina's face as she experienced her own climax. She saw me looking, exposed her teeth and hissed. She relaxed at the same time as my penis stopped spurting. Leaning forward, she kissed me on the lips.

I pulled out of Kabrina, without breaking my kiss with Sharina. I moved onto the bed, pushed her backwards and fell between her opening thighs. Still stiff, I slid into Sharina's slippery organ, but lay unmoving in her cradling arms and thighs.

Her inner muscles rippled gently around my penis, clenched and unclenched with a steady rhythm. I didn't have an orgasm, but it sent gentle waves of pleasure through my whole body.

"Hey," Kabrina said softly beside my ear. "What about me?"

Sharina released me, I moved over into her sister's embrace, slipped back into an eager and hot sheath. They were twins, and it didn't come as a surprise when she continued Sharina's gentle massaging of my penis.

I knew we should be jumping, because contrary to what Kabrina had said…we were on a time-schedule.

But to hell with it, I thought, *this is much more pleasurable.*

Chapter Sixteen

You never knew what your stressed mind would throw at you during a jump. Sometimes nothing but nightmares, at other times replays of past experiences, not always exactly the way they happened.

"I've spotted one of their *Tanks* at the bottom of the ravine half a klick west of our location, sir." Roberts looked up from the spy-screen, adjusted his helmet. "We could hit them easily with one of the *Hawk missiles*."

"We could, but it would alert others in the area to our presence." I checked my laser. It was fully charged. So far, there had been no need to use our weapons. But we couldn't hide forever. One of their scouts would eventually spot us.

We were on the fourth planet in the Capella System, 42 light years away from Sol. Not really a desirable place. The weather was unpredictable, the fluctuations in temperature extreme. No colonist would ever want to settle here, but one of the Search teams discovered unusually large deposits of *Mecka-crystals*, the building blocks for the fuel crystals all jump-ships used to cross the vastness of space.

Unfortunately, humans weren't the only ones who made that discovery.

The Vegans laid claim to the planet the same time the Terrans did.

There had always been an uneasy truth between the Terran Empire and the Vegan-Union. The Vegans discovered space travel long before man and considered themselves superior and with more rights to space real estate.

Their species were rude and loudmouthed, easily provoked. Of reptilian ancestry, they preferred hotter and more humid systems, but had no scruples claiming planets that were suited better to humans. Not because they needed more room to expand, but strictly out of principle.

But this planet was different. It had something both races needed and wanted. We couldn't afford to let them have it. Not only was it rich on *Mecka-crystals*, its location made it a strategic spot to set up a military post.

To make matters worse, the Vegans weren't the only ones who we needed to worry about. It seems the Kapellans also showed an interest. Unless we could settle this quickly, those *Birds* would surely bring a small armada and settle it for us.

"We'll have to wait until Unit K arrives." I watched Kelvin Byrne as he set up his own surveillance system. He was my comm-officer, the best in the field.

As were the others.

Mark Roberts, weapon specialist. Carl Slovaki, the best camouflage-man I've ever met. He could make an *Eagle-transporter* disappear from any spy-screen.

Then there was David Slieman, the best sharpshooter in my unit. He never missed a target, no matter how small or how far. As long as it could be seen.

Raoul Jyndhal, my psych-officer and strategist. He possessed the uncanny ability of predicting enemy movements…better than any computer.

These men were the best and they were loyal. They'd go through the fire for me, without asking for a reason.

"Damn!" Byrne cursed.

"What's the problem?"

"I think we've been spotted." Byrne studied his hologram.

"The *Tank*?" I asked.

"No. They have a *Spy-bird* hidden in the *Glass-forest* 22 degrees north east."

Slieman bent over the hologram. "Want me to take it out, Captain?"

"The Tank has changed direction, sir," Roberts reported. "Looks like they're heading our way."

"Take it out!" I told Slieman.

Slieman grabbed his Mark-Seven and his holo-scope and went outside. We watched it on Byrne's hologram. We couldn't see the *Spy-bird*, but it lit up the whole cube when it was hit by Slieman's projectile.

Slieman appeared inside the Lander moments later. Without speaking, he took his seat, activated the holding magnets. The rest of us had already strapped in. Slovaki finished energizing the *Cloak* that would make us invisible in the Vegan's detector-net.

"Take us up!" I told Hammer, our pilot.

The Jet-Lander shot up. The stabilizers compensated as Five G-forces tried to flatten us in our seats.

"They've launched a *Seeker*." Hammer spoke calmly. "We've

been found."

Ejection Sequence activated. The cold voice of the ship's AI sounded crisp in my comm-speakers as the Defense-System took over controls. I registered the closing of the energy field around my seat, then the sky opened underneath me and I dropped into the alien sky.

Five more shimmering modules appeared beside me. Above us, the Jet-Lander accelerated to escape the *Seeker*, but it was no use. A small miniature sun flared up briefly, then was gone.

Below us, the harsh surface flashed silvery. We might get lucky and land inside a *Glass-forest*, where our chances for survival were much better than in the open. We might just be able to hang on until Unit K arrived with enforcements.

My energy-module landed softly among the glittering trees, opened the same time as the magnetic hold released me from my seat and I stumbled out, laser already in my hand.

I heard the cracking of the brittle tree branches as my comrades joined me on the forest floor.

A soon as Byrne emerged from his module he dropped to his knees to set up his portable detection system. I watched him launch the tiny spy-eye, which would hover above the trees to report the arrival of our enemy. "The Tank is still heading our way," Byrne reported. "Contact in approximately fifteen minutes."

We had nowhere to run, so we spread out and settled in the protection of the giant *Glass-trees*, waiting for the enemy. They couldn't bring their *Tank* in here. It was too big and cumbersome. We were quite safe from the destructive weapons of the *Tank*, because the crystalline structure of the trees prevented the *Tank's* detection net to locate us. The Vegans had no choice but to come in after us.

"The Tank has reached the edge of the forest." Byrne spoke without emotion. He worked the remote to let the tiny spy-satellite get closer to the enemy vehicle.

"Captain?" Roberts' voice came over the comm.

"Yes, Roberts?"

"I could take care of the *Tank*."

I suppressed a grin. I should have known. Roberts carried all kinds of weapons in his backpack. A mini *Hawk-missile* was surely among them. I saw him crouching over his spy-screen, behind one of the trees to my left.

"Do it!" I said.

"Ten enemy soldiers have entered the forest at two o'clock."

Byrne reported.

"Hawk has left the nest," Roberts said calmly.

I barely managed to count to ten before the sound of a loud explosion interrupted the eerie silence of the alien forest.

This forest was unlike any forest I've ever been in. Instead of reducing sounds, the structure of the trees amplified them. My helmet automatically dampened the sound waves, but they were still strong enough to make my ears ring.

The Vegans in the forest would not be happy. Their escape-vehicle had been destroyed and they would be madder than a robot with a short circuit.

The first one arrived within minutes. His saurian face was covered by a protective facemask, only his bulging eyes were visible.

Roberts was the first one to spot him. His laser flashed, but he missed. The Saurian had seen him, too, and he disappeared behind one of the thick tree-trunks.

Then all hell broke lose. Ten bulky figures charged us, their weapons flashing like fireworks on New Year's Eve.

It was over in less than a minute.

The advantage remained on our side. They knew we were inside the forest, but not exactly where.

The Vegans were fierce and fearless soldiers, but they also were overconfident in their abilities and had a tendency to underestimate their enemies. They usually rushed in too soon and without thinking.

I called my men over the comm.

"Roberts?"

"Here."

"Byrne?"

"Here, Cap."

"Slovaki?"

"Yoh, Chief."

"Slieman?"

"Here."

"Hammer?"

"Acknowledged."

"Jyndhal?"

No answer.

"Raoul, are you there?"

Roberts found him slumped against a tree. He was dead. We buried him in the alien ground. Right beside the tree where he had died.

When I walked out of the forest, I saw him standing leaning against one of the crystalline trees. He was smiling.

"You are dead," I said.

"I'm not dead, just sleeping," he said and spread his golden wings.

I hadn't seen him change. His skin gleamed golden in the rays of the alien sun.

"You were never there," I told him.

He chuckled. "I am wherever you are." Spreading his great wings, he soared into the sky.

Chapter Seventeen

Eden's Gate was colonized in the first wave of human expansion. The few bands of indigenous people that roamed the prairies and tundra were ignored, and humans soon flourished on this ideal planet.

The planet isn't named *Eden's Gate* without a reason. The temperature fluctuates between minus 20 degrees and plus 110 degrees Fahrenheit. There are some islands where it never goes below plus 50 degrees, and the hottest it ever gets is 90 degrees. No devastating storms and hurricanes, no active volcanoes, just pleasant weather.

Things grow well on Eden's Gate, mainly all kinds of different spices, herbs and drugs.

Eden's Gate lies close to the outer fringes of known human space and is therefore prone to being invaded by pirates and raiders. However, the planet is rich and can effort modern defense systems. The population is in the range of half a billion people, give or take a few million. There is plenty of room for expansion, the planet is slightly smaller than Earth, with a larger landmass; most of the land is fertile and livable.

Planetary Defense directed us to Tamarak, one of the bigger cities. It has the largest spaceport and is home to many interplanetary trading companies.

We docked in one of the smaller docking bays and hired a maintenance crew to refuel the ship and give it a check-up. I also wanted it to be searched for any bugs that might have been installed before we took possession of the ship.

While the ship was being serviced, the girls and I went to find a company that would sell us what we needed. One of the port-taxis took us to the center of Tamarak where, the driver assured us, we would find a number of trading company headquarters.

Tamarak was like any other city I've seen. Even though Eden's Gate was rich and productive, only the huge conglomerates reaped the profits. The average citizen didn't live any richer than the average citizen on any other planet. We drove through a couple of slum-areas, where poorly dressed people lingered on sidewalks and on porches in need of repairs, where children played with rocks and kicked a ball made from discarded clothing.

I noticed one difference, a great number of people, men and

women, with shaved heads, and long, thin ponytails that hung down to their buttocks.

"What's with all the bald heads? Some kind of epidemic?" I asked the driver.

He snorted. "The *Galactics*. You don't want to deal with them. They believe that the end of the universe is near. Crazy fanatics. I could never understand why someone who was blessed with perfectly good hair would want to shave it off." He lifted his cap to expose a shiny skull. "I wish I had some hair," he complained.

I laughed. "How about a hair-transplant? Or gene manipulation?"

He shook his head. "Can't afford either." Chuckling, he waved a hand. "It's not that important, really. If it weren't for those idiots it probably wouldn't even bother me."

""You hate them that much?" I asked.

"They are troublemakers. Rumor has it they were responsible for our Prime-Director's fatal accident last year. He wanted to pass a law that would outlaw their cult."

"And your new Prime Director?"

He turned his head, lowered his voice when he spoke. "There are rumors that he is one of them. But you didn't hear that from me." He gave me a sharp look. "It's obvious you are from off-world and know nothing about our world, except what our government wants you to know. Take some advice: be careful whom you are dealing with. That's all I have to say."

I nodded. "Well, thanks for the tip. I'll keep it in mind."

"Are there no Galactics on other planets?" the driver asked.

"Plenty," I told him. "But this is the first planet I visit where they shave their heads."

"Really? So how do you recognize them?"

"You don't always. Some worship in secret."

He snorted in disgust. "Doesn't surprise me. Who can figure them out."

He dropped us off in front of the *Starsweeps Establishment,* a hotel where we would stay until we were ready to leave this planet again.

We rented a suite. Sharina paid for it with one of her universal credit-chips. She seemed to carry an endless supply of them in a pouch-belt, which she had strapped around her narrow waist. The suite was luxurious and expensive, but, what the hell, it wasn't my money.

"You girls can go shopping or do whatever women do, I'm going to see if I can make a deal with the place across the street," I told them.

"Are you talking about the *Intergalactic Spice Company?*" Kabrina asked.

"The very same one. I figure with a name like that they should have what we are looking for."

"We'll come with you," Sharina said.

"I can manage by myself."

"I know you can, but it will be more impressive if you come with a couple of assistants."

"On the other hand," her sister said, "Sharina and I *could* go shopping, but not for pretty clothes and cheap jewelry."

"I wasn't …," I protested.

She held up a hand and smiled. "Maybe you weren't, but I don't think you're much different from our males. If it were up to them, females would stay in bed all day, look beautiful and be ready to fuck anytime a male wants to."

"Aren't you?" I grinned.

She hissed and showed me her teeth. "That remark alone betrays you, Thomas." She put her hand against my cheek; I could feel sharp nails digging into my skin. "We are always ready, and you must admit, we know how to please a male, we are experts, but we are capable of doing other things besides coupling. Very capable."

I pulled her hand away. "I don't doubt that," I said. "So tell me, what will you be shopping for?"

"Diamonds. I did some research. Eden's Gate is famous for its beautiful purple diamonds."

"I am aware of that, but aren't they prohibitively expensive?"

She laughed. "We don't need money."

I looked into her strange emerald eyes; they seemed shiny, as if they were glowing with some inner fire. I found no need to ask how she planned to acquire the diamonds. "Just be careful," I warned her, "there is no place to run."

"Same goes for you, Big Man. You have a talent for getting into trouble." She lifted up and kissed me on the lips, then she stepped back and winked, smiling. "See you later; we'll be ready for you when you get back."

Sharina giggled beside her, churning her hips. "Double ready."

I had to shake my head. I had no doubt they were capable of

pulling off whatever they planned. Even though they acted like a pair of empty bubbleheads, they were far from that.

Alien and dangerous, but not stupid.

* * * *

It surprised me to see how little traffic there was. Most of the vehicles that traversed the wide street were tear-shaped. Almost all were just large enough to hold only two people. They floated silently a dozen centimeters above the smooth surface of the street. Opaque windows hid the occupants inside.

The sidewalks were a different story…they held crowds of people. Again, I spotted a large number of shaved heads, male and female.

I crossed the street, headed for the building that housed the Intergalactic Spice Company, tall, mainly steel and glass. The lobby looked plush, richly furnished. On the walls hung expensive paintings. Finely carved statues stood in corners and niches.

I walked up to the ornate desk, smiled at the woman seated behind it. "My name is Thomas Stone," I said. "I'd like to talk to someone about a purchase of your spices."

She looked me over. Even the huge glasses she wore couldn't hide the icy chill of her eyes. On an advanced planet, like Eden's Gate, people didn't need to wear glasses, eyes could be re-grown or transplanted. Her glasses were purely fashion.

"We only deal in large quantities," she said frostily.

I gave her my best smile. "So do I."

"Just a moment." She looked at the built-in screen on her desk. "I think Senjar Ornez is free. Take a seat while you wait."

I nodded and found myself a comfortable chair.

Most of the paintings were landscapes. There were some that showed spectacular views of the planet from space. One painting caught my curiosity, a three-dimensional portrait of a golden, black-winged man. Whoever painted it was very artistic. The eyes of the man glowed with a lifelike quality and I almost expected him to step out of the picture at any moment. He had one hand clenched into a fist, resting over his heart, the other one lifted high above his head. The scepter it held radiated golden light.

A small statue, almost identical to the painting, stood in one of the niches.

I was just about to get up and take a closer look at the statue when one of the elevator doors opened and a young woman stepped out. Smiling, she walked toward me. I rose to my feet, smiled back at her.

"You must be Senjar Stone," she said in a pleasant voice, held out a hand.

"Guilty," I said and shook her hand. She had a firm grip.

"I am Dorles Rodrego, assistant to Senjar Omez. Please, follow me."

The elevator took us up to the 20th floor. I followed the woman down a carpeted corridor into a plush office. It held a desk with a smooth, polished top, the legs carved from some rich looking local wood. A couple of chairs and a comfortable looking couch finished the decor.

"Can I offer you some refreshments? A glass of wine, perhaps? We have excellent wines, which we also export, by the way." She sat down behind the desk, leaned back in her chair, looked at me out of dark, brooding eyes. "Well?" she asked.

"Sorry," I said. I had been staring at her breasts, which were clearly visible under her transparent blouse. "I'll have a glass of wine, if it is not too much trouble."

She smiled, shook a lock of hair out of her face. "No trouble," she said, then she looked up and spoke into the air, "Bring us a bottle of *Lavender Bloom* and two glasses."

It didn't take more than thirty seconds when a door behind her opened and a young girl walked through, carrying a tray with a bottle, two glasses, and a plate full of cookies. She didn't say anything, sat the tray down on the desk and walked out again. I noticed the long braid of hair that hung down her back.

On one of the walls hung another painting of the golden winged man. Dorles Rodrego saw me looking at it, smiled. "The Golden Lightbringer," she said. "I guess it is plain that I am a worshipper."

Shrugging, I said, "Your religious beliefs are not my concern." I studied her beautiful face and admired the thick, luxurious hair that hung loosely past her shoulders. "You don't have a shaved head," I observed.

She ran a hand through her hair, pushed it back. "It is not required. I deal with people from other planets, some do not approve of our beliefs." Her dark eyes bored into mine. "Do you, Senjar Stone?"

"Like I said, I don't care one way or another, as long as it doesn't interfere with business." I lifted my glass and took a sip from the wine, smooth, dry, with a pleasant aroma. I looked at her. "Are you authorized to make deals or are you just entertaining me, Senjarina Rodrego?"

"Both, Senjar Stone. Business need not be boring." She smiled enticingly. "But first I'd like to know a little more about you. What kind of quantities are you looking for and what would you like to buy?"

I spread my hands. "I'll be honest with you. I know nothing about the spice business." I reached into my coat pocket, pulled out a wallet, took out the little rod it contained. "Here, these are my credentials, everything you need to know about me, the type and size of my ship, my credit rating, everything."

She took the little rod from my fingers, caressed it gently. "Everything?" she asked.

"Pretty much." I nodded, smiled. "Of course, some things you may have to find out for yourself."

She pushed the little rod into her computer, studied the screen. Her eyes widened slightly for a moment, a frown creased her forehead, the she smiled, looked at me. "Everything seems to be in order. So, what is it you are looking for?"

"I need to fill the storage rooms in my ship. I leave it up to you. I trust you will sell me only the kind of spices that are in demand. This could be the beginning of a profitable relationship."

"I see." She chewed thoughtfully on her lower lip, while her long fingers moved efficiently across the input screen. "There," she said after awhile. "I've relayed your order to our shipping department. It is not far from the spaceport. Loading should begin within a couple of hours." She looked at me with eyes veiled by long lashes. "Now that business has been taken care of, how about another glass of wine?"

She came around the desk, sat on the edge and poured from a long-necked bottle, filling my glass. Her skirt had a slit from her waist down; it parted, exposed a long, slim thigh, part of her hip.

I drank my second glass too fast, felt slightly lightheaded. That glass contained more than just alcohol. Soft music played from hidden speakers. I suddenly looked at her exposed breasts. Smiling, she stood in front of me. With slow movements she pushed her skirt past her hips, let it pool around her ankles. She wore only a tiny, transparent pair of panties.

"Take them off," she crooned. When I hooked my fingers into the elastic waistband, she shook her head. "With your teeth."

Kneeling in front of her, I took the thin material between my teeth, pulled down gently. My nose scraped her smooth belly, sank into her moist slit. I smelled the perfumed aroma of her hairless womanhood.

"Use your tongue," she whispered haughtily and pushed her hips forward. Her hands grabbed my head, held it.

She tasted salty, but pleasant.

Moaning, she pulled away. "Get undressed," she told me, her breath coming in little gasps. Watching me take off my clothes, she played with herself, her black eyes never leaving my face.

When I stood naked, she sat on the desk, her thighs wide open. I moved between them, pushed my erect member into her waiting orifice. She felt wet and soft. I entered her deeply, crushed my mouth to hers to quell her loud gasp. Putting my hands under her fleshy buttocks and, without uncoupling, I carried her to the couch. Then I put her onto her back and began to pound between her clutching thighs.

I made her come a few times, but held back for the final moment.

Passionate and wild, she rode me with unashamed abandon when she was on top, bucked like an animal in heat when she knelt in front of me. I grabbed her gyrating hips, pulled her buttocks into my lap and held her tight while I erupted inside her quaking sex-canal. She screamed, quivered in my grasp as her own warm juices flowed out of her.

I should have been more aware, but my mind was still cloudy from the wine and the drug.

They were on me before I could free my spurting penis. I had not seen them coming, never even heard the opening door.

Chapter Eighteen

I don't remember anything about the world or myself before Elesia Stone found me on that obscure planet. When I joined the Terran Space Force, I began my career right at the bottom, like any other cadet. Part of my training included unarmed combat. It came to me easily, and it wasn't long before my skills surpassed everyone else's, including the skills of my instructor.

I am stronger and faster than anyone I know. All that doesn't help much when you get knocked on the head with a blunt instrument.

How long I stayed unconscious, I don't know, but when I regained my senses I was lying helplessly bound on the floor, still naked. There were three assailants, all of them big, with bald heads and long ponytails. Dorles Rodrego sat behind her desk, properly dressed and looking very business-like.

She must have been watching me, because when I opened my eyes, she asked, "How do you feel, Commodore Stone?" Her smile looked cold, unpleasant.

Groaning, I shook my head, trying to get rid of the buzzing in my ears.

"Didn't I satisfy you?" I asked.

One of the thugs kicked me in the ribs. "Show some respect for the Senjarina," he growled.

I can take pain, but this bastard really kicked me hard. Wincing, I still managed a grin. "You seemed to enjoy it," I said, still looking at Dorles.

"Whatever gave you that idea? I hated every moment of it."

"You certainly fooled me, especially since you're the one who came on to me," I said.

"Liar!" she spat. "You raped me!"

This did not look good. I had a feeling I was being set up for something. She called me *Commodore*; she knew exactly who I was.

"Get him out of here!" she told the three who were watching me as if I were some kind of disease-carrying animal. Two of them picked me up and carried me out of the door, down the empty corridor toward the back and into a freight-elevator. I noticed that the third one carried my clothing.

"This is a mistake, you know." I tried to make conversation.

"Whatever they're paying you, I'll pay you triple."

"For what?" growled the one who had kicked me. He seemed to be their leader.

"For not killing me."

He actually laughed. "Who said that we'll kill you?" he asked.

"Aren't you?"

"We don't kill people. We leave that to others."

They didn't quite convince me, especially when we exited on a floor below ground. We seemed to be in an underground garage. They threw me into the dark interior of some delivery-vehicle, and after a few moments, I knew we were traveling. Soon after that, we were air-born.

I tried to loosen my bonds, but they had done a good job, so I just relaxed. After what seemed like hours, the motion of the vehicle stopped. I blinked into the bright glare of the opening door, and then they pulled me out of my prison and dumped me unceremoniously onto a muddy ground. They threw a bundle on top of me and left me lying in the dirt.

Someone had cut the ropes that held my wrists together, but the bastards never cut the rope around my ankles.

I became aware of a nauseating smell and realized that I was in a garbage dump. My boots were among the bundle of stuff they had thrown on top of me, and when I examined them, I found my combat-knife still strapped to my right boot.

These guys either were amateurs or just didn't care. Obviously, they didn't want me dead, otherwise I would be, and I thanked my lucky stars for this little bit of fortune.

The foul-smelling liquid I lay in covered my body, and I used my shiny black shirt to rub myself dry. Then I put on my pants and threw my coat over my naked upper body. After wiping my feet with my shirt, I slipped into my boots and felt better immediately.

Searching through my coat, I discovered that my wallet with all my credit chips and my ID was gone.

Damn! I had no idea where I was and no money to get anywhere. They even found the tiny communicator that I carried behind the lapel of my coat.

These guys had been professionals, after all.

The stench started getting to me. I had to get away from this place. There wasn't much daylight left, actually none, I realized, because the sun was a huge red ball, half of it already sinking below the horizon.

Silhouetted against the disappearing ball of red fire were the towers and squat buildings of a nearby town or village.

Rolling my, hopefully not ruined, silky shirt into a small bundle I set out toward what could be my first step to getting back to my hotel. The town didn't seem far away, but getting there proved to be rough. I kept slipping in the foul smelling muck that covered the dump. There were heaps of garbage strewn haphazardly around the landscape, and I had to find a passable road between them.

When I got closer to the town, I saw that the buildings were crumbling and falling apart. What once had been tall, smooth-walled towers were nothing but empty ruins, the glass in the round windows broken a long time ago. The expected help was, obviously, not to be found in this place, but maybe it would provide shelter and protection from the cool wind that began to blow.

I just skirted a small mountain of rusted metal when I became aware of someone or something stalking me. When I turned around, I caught movement out of the corner of my eye. Then a black, skeletal creature stepped into my view.

The yellow, glowing eyes were the first thing I saw, below them a long nose, like the beak of a bird, and a stubby snout with long, gleaming teeth. The creature's bony arms ended in long fingers, tipped with wicked looking curved nails.

At first, I thought it wore a black cloak, until the cloak spread open to reveal itself as a pair of black leathery wings.

Emitting a piercing cry, the winged creature took to the air, shot straight toward me. I ducked, barely avoiding the sweep of the claws. My hand went down to my boot. I felt the reassuring smooth hilt of my combat-knife. Whipping it out, I rolled away from the spot I had been standing on.

The blade glowed with white fire as the hilt recognized the pattern of my palm. It could slice through steel as easily as flesh and bone. I came up, lifting my left arm to protect my neck, at the same time stabbing with my right at the shadow swooping down. I heard a ripping sound as the 30 cm blade penetrated thick skin and tore apart soft flesh underneath. I gave the blade a vicious twist, pulled it free, stabbed again.

With a heavy thud, a dark body hit the ground beside me. Suddenly, the sound of furiously beating wings ripped the air asunder. I counted at least two dozen of the creatures swooping out of the sky.

I severed the clawed hand of one of them, shredded the wings of another one, but they kept on coming. A sharp claw ripped through my coat, tearing the tough material. I felt the razor-sharp nails cut my skin, but ignored the sudden pain.

A darkness welled up inside me, took over my body. My eyes seemed to look through a red haze, but my vision stayed clear. Time slowed down, everything happened in slow motion.

I rolled and thrust upwards, kicked a creature in the head with my right foot, heard bones crack, smashed my left fist into a snarling face, while at the same time laying open a wrinkled belly, spilling purple guts into the dirt.

The attacks stopped as suddenly as they had begun. Dead and mortally wounded bodies lay everywhere. The surviving creatures formed a ring around me, but kept their distance. I took a deep breath, winced when I became aware of the pain in my back. The red haze I had been looking through was gone. I knew they would not attack again.

"What are you?" one of the creatures asked with a voice like rusted hinges.

"I am a man," I said.

"Not human," croaked another one.

I laughed. "I am human, just a little different. Why did you attack me?"

"Meat. We are hungry." The first speaker answered.

I looked at the dead bodies on the ground. "You have plenty to eat now," I said and began walking forward. They backed away, but kept me in their circle.

"Need human meat," he said.

I chuckled. "Then you go hungry. You said it yourself…I am not human. My meat might poison you."

"It will be dark soon, very dark," announced another gravelly voice. "Human eyes are weak in the dark."

I noticed that the red disk of the sun was almost gone, and shadows were long and black. Maybe my estimation had been wrong; maybe they would rush me after dark. I motioned with the burning blade of my knife. "This is no ordinary weapon," I said. "It will find your flesh, even if I can't see you."

A brilliant light flared up suddenly behind them, some of them covered their eyes against the glare. Cries of pain filled the air. I heard a small explosion, one of the winged men tumbled to the ground, kicking, his head gone, only the bloody stump of his long neck remained. Another one fell with a huge hole in his bony chest.

"Leave!" commanded a booming voice.

The creatures milled around, hesitating for a moment. A third explosion and another headless body decided their next move. They took to the air, flapped away on their leathery wings.

"Are you alright, stranger?" The voice was definitely female, even though it was distorted by an electronic amplifier.

I watched the dark shadowy figure come closer. She was slim, tall, dressed in a black, loose body suit. In one hand she carried a bow, in the other a small conical device, probably the loudspeaker. Her eyes swept over the lifeless bodies around me, then she stared at me. "You did this?"

I nodded, bent down to wipe the blade of my knife on one of the bodies, sheathed it. When I straightened out, she was still staring at me. "You did this with only a knife? What are you?" she asked.

I grinned. "The second time somebody wants to know that tonight. I'll give you the same answer. I am a man, my name is Thomas Stone."

She shook her head. "No man I know could have done this. What are you doing out here in the dark? This place is not safe; the *Ghouls* are the least dangerous."

"I assume these creatures are the Ghouls." I made a sweeping motion with my hand.

She stared at me again. "You have never encountered them before?"

"No. I'm not from around here. Just visiting."

"You're an off-worlder. That explains it. You *look* human."

I squinted at the bright light still shining into my face and eyes. "Please, tell your friend to aim that thing somewhere else. I'm going blind."

She yelled something over her shoulder, the circle of light moved to illuminate the dead creatures on the ground. She bent down do examine one whose arm I had sliced off. "This is no ordinary knife you're carrying," she observed.

"No. It's a *Disrupter*. Only the military are allowed to have them," I explained.

"Yet you possess one. You are a military man, then?"

I shook my head. "Not anymore." I pointed to the bow and the quiver she carried on her back. "Those are no ordinary arrows."

She smiled. "It seems we both carry illegal weapons. The arrowheads explode on impact."

"What if one of them had hit me?"

"You'd be without a head." She laughed. "I never miss my target. Neither does Terrex."

"Your partner?"

"My brother." She cocked her head, listened to something, then she said, "Come, we better get moving and seek shelter. The Ghouls will be back with reinforcement. Besides, all this meat will attract the carrion-eaters."

She turned, began to walk away. I followed her slowly. The wound in my back burned fiercely. I needed to have someone take a look at it.

Terrex turned out to be a young boy, probably about fourteen standard years old. He looked thin, like his sister. His hair hung long and unkempt. An ugly scar ran down the left side of his face. Nothing that could not be repaired, if you had the money to pay for it.

He grinned and looked at me with obvious admiration. "Where are you from?" he asked me.

I pointed into the sky. "Far away from here."

"I've never been to the stars," he said, dreamily. "What's it like?"

"Most inhabited planets are like yours. The animals and plants may be different, but the people are all the same." I smiled grimly. "You can't trust anyone."

"You can trust us," he said, and I knew that he spoke the truth.

"Hey, you two," the girl interrupted, "get moving, unless you want to be fodder for the *Shakkels*."

I looked into the direction she pointed and saw dark shapes slinking silently between the mountains of garbage. She started jogging toward the ruins of the town. The boy dimmed his light, began to trek after her. I felt suddenly very tired, but I managed to stay with them. Without the light, it would have been hard to see. This planet had no moon and the visible stars were too dim.

The girl led us to a squat building that looked almost untouched by whatever destroyed most of the dwellings. "We will be safe in here," she explained as we slipped through a doorway that could still be closed with a heavy metal door. The hinges creaked in defiance, as she shut the door behind us, but the lock clicked smoothly into place.

Chapter Nineteen

We were in a large room. Once there had been windows, but they were now barred by thick sheets of rusted metal. Furs were piled up in a corner, clay pots and cups in another. I saw some backpacks beside the pile of furs.

"Welcome to our home away from home," the girl said and walked over to one of the walls to turn on a portable atomic torch. Suddenly bright light flooded the room "I hate the dark," she said. "Now, let me look at you a little closer."

She came up to me, peered into my eyes. I noticed that hers were of a deep purple color; her pupils were slit, like those of a cat.

"You are not human," I observed.

She laughed, shook her short, curly hair. "I never claimed that I was." She wrinkled her nose. "You stink, let's get you cleaned up. We have water."

I took off my coat. Her eyes widened a little when she looked me over.

"You are very muscular," she murmured, a pink tongue running over her red lips. She dug long fingers into my biceps, ran her hand down my back. I winced when she touched my wounds.

"What is it?" she asked.

"Those Ghouls have sharp claws," I said.

She gasped when she looked at my back. "These wounds," she said. "A lesser man would have fainted by now."

Terrex brought a clay-bowl filled with clean water. The girl rummaged inside one of the backpacks, brought out strips of cloth and a small metal jar. Very carefully she washed my back. She had gentle, soft hands. Hard to imagine that they were capable of pulling a bow.

She applied a salve from the metal jar; it stung, but soon the pain subsided, and I began to feel normal again.

"Too bad your beautiful coat is ruined," she said and added, "Your pants don't look too clean, either."

"Want me to take them off?" I asked, not really meaning it.

She lowered her eyelids. Long black lashes hid her cat's eyes. I noticed her beautiful face, narrow, with high cheekbones, her lips full and pouting.

Smiling, she licked her lips again. "Later. Let's have something to eat first," she purred. "I am quite hungry."

Terrex squatted already on the floor, munching on something.

Searching through her pack again, the girl brought out a plastic bottle and a wrapped package. She opened it, revealing brown rolls of baked dough. She offered one to me. I bit off a piece, discovered meat and vegetables inside. The meat was tough, but it didn't taste bad.

She spread one of the furs, lowered herself onto it. Sitting cross-legged, she padded the spot in front of her. "Come, join me."

Gratefully, I sat down, finding myself quite tired. She took a swig from her bottle, and then held it out to me. "Drink," she said. Thanking her, I put the bottle to my lips and almost gagged when the liquid ran down my parched throat. "What the hell is this?" I croaked.

She burst out laughing. Behind me, Terrex joined his sister in her laughter.

"*Swark-milk*," she said.

"It tastes sour."

"It is quite popular with my people. We let it ferment to give it a bit of a kick. It will put you to sleep if you drink too much."

"There is no chance of that, thank you." I handed the bottle back to her. "I'll drink water, if you don't mind."

She drank some more, burped and wiped her mouth with the back of her hand. Her purple eyes were large when she looked at me. "It also makes your blood heat up with desire and gives a man power over a woman." Her hand reached toward me. With her finger she traced the outlines of my lips. "She'll do anything he wants," she whispered.

"In that case, maybe I should give it one more chance. It won't kill me, right?"

Her smile revealed tiny, sharp teeth. "It is not the Swark-milk you should worry about."

The liquid felt like raw fire going down my throat, but it did warm me up from the inside, and after awhile it seemed as if bypassed my stomach and went straight into my penis. Good thing I still had my pants on.

"What were you doing out there?" I asked her.

"Hunting."

"At night?"

"We heard and saw the Ghouls, and we knew that there was a battle going on. We came to investigate."

"But what exactly are you doing here?"

"Like I said, hunting."

"For what?"

She shrugged. "The rich people in the city throw away many things. We need many things. So we search the dumping places for treasures."

"Like that torch on the wall and the light Terrex is carrying."

"I think I understand."

Her eyes searched my face. "Do you really?" she asked. "I will never be able to live in a big city, in a fancy home, or mingle with the humans, except as a slave. And do you know why? Because as far as the humans are concerned we are animals, even though we are part human. We have no rights. We are not allowed to own property. We *are* property."

"Where do you live?"

Her arm swept the room. "The free members of my kind live in places like this, or in rundown areas at the outskirts of big cities where the law-enforcers don't dare to go. But most of my people live in the wild forests or in the mountains." She smiled. "We are wild, but not uncivilized. We have our own codes and laws. Our dwellings may not be fancy, but they are clean and comfortable, hidden away from prying human eyes. Yet, there are some of my people who actually live among humans, after altering their bodies and wearing artificial lenses to hide their eyes."

""You said you are part human?"

"My ancestors are the real owners of this world. They lived here before the humans came. They called themselves *Children of the Dust*. Ironic, isn't it? Because that's what they are now: Dust. Even though the humans declared them animals, they had no problem capturing the females of the *Children* and using them to satisfy their sexual lust. We are the result. As the offspring of those unions grew and multiplied the pure members of the *Children of the Dust* became fewer and fewer, until they were all gone."

"Are there many of you?"

Her eyes were lazy when she looked at me. I noticed that she had taken off her soft-soled boots. She had long toes, almost like fingers. She reached out with one foot, trailed a long toe down my naked chest.

"Many," she murmured. "More than they know."

"The humans, you mean?"

Smiling, she revealed small fangs. "Someday we will surprise them," she said. Her foot moved down. I felt those long toes in my crotch. Looking over to where Terre sat, I saw that he had his eyes closed. He seemed to be asleep.

She saw me looking, laughed deep in her throat. "He doesn't care who I couple with, even though I initiated him myself. Jealousy is not one of our weaknesses."

"You had sexual intercourse with your brother?" I asked, not really shocked.

"The nights can get long and lonely," she said. "Tell me, how did you end up in this place?"

"A business-deal gone wrong. I was warned against dealing with the Galactics."

"You should have heeded that warning. The Galactics are ruthless fanatics. They hunt us down, because we reject their teachings; but they do not mind keeping young males and females of our species as slaves. Human males like our exotic bodies." With a fluid movement she ran a hand down the front of her suit. It split open, revealed a light-skinned body. Rising, she let the top of her black outfit fall down to her waist, then she slipped the bottom part past her slim hips and pulled her muscular legs out of the leggings.

Naked, she stood in front of me, her legs slightly apart. The loose top of her suit had hidden her upper body. She had two fair-sized breasts, with thick, short nipples. Below each breast she had a series of smaller bumps running down her chest and past the spot where her navel should have been.

I counted four rudimentary breasts with tiny nipples on each side.

Below her flat belly, she displayed a thick dark triangle. Turning around, she presented her round buttocks. I stared at the finger-long thin tail that grew from the base of her spine. She laughed softly and wiggled it. Then she faced me again, dropped to her knees in front of me and began tugging on my pants.

I didn't need much more encouragement. My erect penis already strained painfully to get out. I leaned back and let her pull down my pants. Then she climbed on top of me. Hovering for a moment with her hairy sex-organ almost touching my penis, she grabbed it and guided in into that thick bush. She was as ready as I was. Wet and creamy, she sheathed my member. She felt tight, and even though she was slippery, it took a moment for me to enter her fully.

"I expected you to be big," she moaned, "but you are a delightful surprise." Slowly she moved up and down, and I groaned when the pleasure began to run through my body.

She came almost immediately. A guttural sound escaped her open mouth as she experienced her first orgasm.

I studied her two rows of breasts as she churned her slim body on top of me. Reaching out, I cupped both upper breasts with my hands, felt them quiver under my touch. They were soft, but solid, with a slightly conical tilt to them.

The gouges in my back began to burn as my sweat flowed into them.

"Lift up and turn around," I told the girl.

Reluctantly, she freed my penis, knelt beside me. "Hurry," she said with a breathless whisper.

Crouching above her, I guided my member between her soft buttocks. Her little tail curled to the side, exposing the cleft below her puckering anus. Reaching between her legs, she grabbed my penis, pulled it forward. Then I slipped back into her hot slippery sheath.

No problem this time.

Clamping my hands around her slim hips, I moved steadily between her clutching buttocks. She bucked and purred beneath me, coming several times. Then I couldn't hold it back any longer. With a suppressed cry I erupted, held her in a tight grip until I stopped coming. We fell sideways. Still buried inside her, I put my arm around her and lay there, listening to her ragged breathing.

"Even this I didn't expect," she said softly after her breathing became normal. "Not so long ago I was a servant in one of the human households. The head of the House liked me more than his wife, who was older. I hated his touch, but he never lasted long. A few strokes and he was finished. And none of his male friends, who used me, were any different. But you..."

I chuckled into her short, soft hair. "I've surprised many women."

I fell asleep, satisfied and tired.

Chapter Twenty

I awoke to a darkened room.

Somebody had dimmed the lights. I felt chilly, got up, took another fur from the pile and went back to my sleeping place. The girl lay curled up in the fetal position. I lay down beside her, pulled the fur over our bodies. She stirred, stretched and turned to face me.

"Are you asleep?" she whispered, yawned.

"No. Sorry, I woke you, but I thought you may be cold," I whispered back.

She snuggled up to me, pressed her naked body against mine. I felt her breasts soft against my chest. With gentle fingers she stroked my hip.

It wasn't long before my rod stirred between my legs. She giggled and opened her legs to let my erect member slide between her thighs. Squeezing them together, she suddenly let go, rolled onto her back and spread her legs wide.

I didn't need an invitation. Fully awake now, my eyes had adjusted to the darkness. Throwing off the furs that covered us, I moved between her open thighs. She pulled up her legs and hooked her feet behind her head. Her sex-organ was pushed up, her cleft slightly open, ready to receive my solid pole.

I penetrated her easily this time and pushed myself deep into her. Her arms went around my back, held me in a tight grip to her. Only our lower bodies moved, her buttocks slamming up into my thrusting hips.

I felt ready to explode inside her when the outer door to the building burst open and a bright light flooded over us, exposing our locked bodies to the view of whoever held the light.

Not knowing what to expect I froze, squinted into the glare.

"Don't stop on account of us," laughed a male voice. "I've seen animals fuck before. Go ahead, finish up."

"Hunters!" the girl gasped and pushed me off. I rolled onto my back, my penis sticking into the air like a rocket ready to blast off. The girl crouched beside me, hissing loudly.

"Careful," warned the intruder. "No threatening moves. We have *Burners* aimed at you and we won't hesitate to use them. But we would prefer you whole and alive."

As far as I could make out there were two of them. They took a few more steps into the room. Through the open door behind them, I could see daylight streaming in. Another figure blocked the opening moments later.

"Hey, Bellings," the newcomer called, "What did you find?"

Bellings laughed. "A nest of them. They were just in the act of making more *Katres.*"

"I see them," the new guy said. "That female, she's got a mark on her shoulder. She's an escaped slave. I know that sign, she belongs to the *House of Bluestone.* We'll get a good reward for her." He stepped past the other two. He was big and ugly, with a thick mustache and a bushy beard. Looking at me with cold, narrowed eyes he cursed, then grinned. "Look at that, we've got ourselves a Katre-lover here. This guy is human, at least he looks human."

The bright light they shone into my eyes blinded me, and I couldn't see them clearly, but I saw the heavy, stubby rifle the big guy aimed casually at me.

"Now that you've discovered that I am human what are you going to do?" I asked, keeping my voice level. I could feel the cold Darkness rise inside me again. I knew someone was going to die in the next few moments.

The man named Bellings laughed. "The female, we're going to have some fun with, since you didn't seem to have finished what you started. You...I guess we're just going to have to kill you."

The one with the beard reached down to his wide belt, unclipped something. "Keep the light on them," he said. The small device in his hand flared up. He walked past us, let his light play across the large room. "Here's another one," he announced.

I had been wondering what had happened to Terrex. When I looked, I saw the boy lying flat on the floor, half his body hidden by one of the furs.

"Leave him alone," the girl beside me called out. "He's just a boy."

"Come out from under there," the big man told Terrex.

Slowly the boy crawled forward, crouched on all fours and looked up at the bearded man. With an ugly laugh the big man kicked the boy hard in the side. Terrex rolled with the kick, screamed defiantly and launched himself at his tormenter. The man stepped aside, and with a vicious blow brought the butt of his weapon down on the boy's head.

Terrex crashed to the floor, lay unmoving. The big man leveled his weapon. "Damn filth!" he cursed. "I'll blow your head right off."

Beside me, the girl screamed defiantly. I saw the bow in her hand, didn't wait to see what happened next. I located the boot that held my knife. With a fluid motion I pulled it out of its sheath. The man holding the bright light shifted its aim when Terrex attacked his partner. I could see his head and neck, all I needed. I threw my knife, already moving toward Bellings.

The small explosion from the girl's arrow that took off the bearded man's head echoed through the room when I made contact with Bellings. He didn't have time to react. I drove my stiffened fingers into his larynx, crushing it. Gurgling, he fell at the same time as the man holding the light.

I bent down to pull my knife out of the man's neck, wiped the bloody blade on his jacket. Turning slowly around, I saw the girl bending over her brother. "How is he?" I asked. My voice sounded strange in my ears, hollow, distant.

She looked at me and shrank back, staring. "Your eyes," she said.

"*What* about my eyes?"

"They glow," she whispered. "Like the eyes of a night-hunter. What are you?"

A shiver ran through my body. I looked down at myself, saw blood on my chest, but it wasn't mine.

"I don't really know," I told her truthfully.

She rose. The light had rolled away from the dead man. It illuminated her tall, lithe body. She looked beautiful, even by human standards. The rows of secondary breasts only enhanced her appeal.

Her eyes were large, scared.

I smiled. "Only my enemies need to fear me. Not you." I looked down at Terrex. "How is your brother?"

"He is breathing." She dropped her gaze to her bloodstained hands. "He is bleeding from his head, but I don't think he is badly hurt."

"Good," I said. "Watch the door, there may be more of them." I went to put on my pants, slipped into my boots. Looking at my torn coat, I kicked it into a corner. Then I studied Belling's body. He was about my size. I pulled off his jacket and put it on, almost a perfect fit.

The girl came up beside me. "Let me see your back," she said.

I turned, let her lift up the jacket. Her hand ran down my back. "As I suspected," she said. "Almost healed."

"I've always been a fast healer," I told her.

She shook her head. "You are like no man I have ever seen. You killed two heavily armed men with just a knife and your hands."

"No great feat. They were amateurs. I am a soldier, a professional killer."

"They were killers, also," she said softly.

"Get dressed," I told her and grinned. "Too bad we never finished."

Her smile seemed almost shy. "Another time, perhaps, but not here. There is too much death in this place."

I watched her getting dressed, watched her pale buttocks disappear inside the black body suit. When she turned, the light streaming in through the open doorway illuminated her four pairs of breasts. Then she closed the front of her suit, to my regret. Her alien body made my loins throb with desire, even after killing two men.

I thought of Sharina and her sister when, after killing the Thorans, they told me that killing always made them horny.

Looks like they were not the only ones.

A shadow blocking the doorway made me reach for my knife.

Chapter Twenty-one

I watched the man enter the room, tall and slim, like the girl. When his eyes fell on me, he lifted the crossbow he carried.

"No, Lotar, he is a friend," the girl cried out, stepping in front of me.

"He is a Hunter," Lotar growled. "Step aside."

"No Hunter. He's an off-worlder. He did this."

Lotar looked at the dead bodies on the ground, then at me. "Why are you helping us?" he asked.

"She helped me." I said.

He snorted. "I can imagine how." Walking into the room, his gaze fell on the still body of the boy. "Terrex!" he called out with an anguished voice.

"The Hunter hurt him, but he is not dead," the girl explained.

Lotar rushed to the boy's side, squatted beside him. When he touched him, Terrex stirred. "Are you alright, little brother?" Lotar asked.

Terrex sat up, held his head. "It hurts," he complained. He saw the headless, blood-covered body of the Hunter on the ground beside him. "I thought I was done for. What happened?"

"Don't talk, you're safe now." Lotar rose, glared at me. "I don't trust any human," he said. "I'll be watching you."

"Don't mind my brother," the girl said to me. "He doesn't believe that I was never really mistreated by the Lord I served. In his mind all humans are evil."

"They are. If it were different, they would not keep slaves. And your wonderful Lord used you against your will; is that not being mistreated?" Lotar spat.

"If it helps, I don't believe in slavery, either," I said. "Every living creature has the right to be free."

"Animals, too?" he growled. "Because we are animals."

"Aren't we all?" I smiled. "Some of us are just a little more intelligent."

He gave me a long, brooding look, and then he bent down to pick up one of the rifles. "These should serve us well," he said, glared at me again. "The day will come when the rightful owners of this world will reclaim their birthright."

I shrugged. "None of this is really my concern. I have my own problems. All I want right now is to get back to my ship and get the hell off this planet."

"One less human we'll have to kill," Lotar said.

"Where is Liko?" the girl asked.

"Dead."

"How? He was the best with the bow."

"Bows are no match for energy-rifles. We need better weapons." Lotar spat at Belling's body, and then gave it a vicious kick. "But we did kill two of them. Tersten, Tremar, and Kor are searching for others. Usually there are six to eight in a hunting party."

"We'll have to get away from here. By tomorrow this place will be swarming with Enforcers."

Lotar nodded. "What about him?" He acted as if I didn't exist anymore.

"He's lost. He needs our help."

"Since when does a human need our help?"

"If it weren't for him Terrex and I would be dead." Her eyes bored into his. "You have to learn to be more tolerant, Lotar. A leader has to have the ability to adapt and change, if the need arises. Are you such a man, my brother?"

He brushed her aside. "What does a woman know about how to lead men?" he growled. His cat's eyes burned as he stared at me. "Don't betray us, human. Do not betray her. I failed her once, I will not again. Do you understand?"

I nodded slowly. The hilt of my knife pulsed in my hand. He didn't know how close he had come to dying. His cause might be true, but he was a hothead. I've met men like him before, most of them dead now. When he turned his back to me, I stooped and sheathed my knife, contempt rising inside me. You never turn your back on your enemy, and he considered me as one.

I had no quarrel with him or his kind, but I would have had no qualms killing him, had he given me cause.

Outside, the sun rose into a cloudless sky. It would be a hot day. The three corpses inside the room would betray their presence shortly.

The ruins of the dead city didn't look any friendlier in the daylight. Moss and climbing vines covered the gray, crumbling walls, crawled into the buildings through holes, which at one time had been windows. Only a terrible war could have caused such damage to a once proud city.

Two figures came trotting down the main road. They had bows slung across their backs, but in their hands they carried energy-rifles.

They weren't any friendlier toward me than Lotar.

"Who is he?" one asked.

"A friend." I smiled. "My name is Thomas Stone."

"He's an off-worlder," Terrex said beside me.

"A human," the other one growled.

"Where is Kersten?" Lotar asked.

"He's bringing the boat."

"Go and remove all of our stuff out of the shelter. We must leave no evidence of our stay here," Lotar ordered. "Then leave the door open, the carrion-eaters will take care of the rest."

Moments later, an oblong shaped object came sweeping out of the sky.

An airboat.

I helped to load their belongings into the airboat. I saw similar designs on other planets. They were strictly planet-bound, not built for high altitude, but functional and normally quite safe.

Normally. When I looked into the interior of the boat, I had my doubts. It was loaded with junk.

The girl noticed my interest and smiled. "We had a good hunt," she said. "All of this is useful equipment."

I didn't see any room for passengers.

"I think I'll walk," I said.

"Good idea," Lotar grunted behind me.

"Nobody is walking," the girl said sharply. "If he walks, I walk!"

"I'm not telling you what to do. Do whatever you want."

"You go with your people," I told the girl. "Just tell me which is the fastest way to get back to Tamarok."

The girl was about to reply when the clatter of hoofs on stone made her swing around. I saw two riders appear out of a side street, one of them tall and slim, the other one shorter, stockier.

"Trembor and Rack!" she exclaimed.

The two newcomers drew rein and dismounted. I stared fascinated at the animals they were riding. I knew what they were, but I had never seen a live horse, only on computer displays. Horses were extinct on Earth.

The two men gave me the same look the others gave me, but didn't make any comments.

"We found a stack of energy-packs, fully charged," the taller one said to Lotar. "They are too heavy for our animals. Can you take them?"

"We could," Lotar said, glancing at the girl. "Why don't you and Rack load all you stuff into the boat and come with us. Give your mounts to Renha, my hardheaded sister, here. She insists on helping her human lover."

"We hadn't planned on going back, yet."

"We ran into a group of Hunters, had to kill them. This place won't be safe for awhile," Lotar told them. "The sooner we get far away from here the better it will be."

"Alright." The tall rider looked at the girl. "Take good care of that horse. I'm fond of it." He turned back to Lotar. "What about the Hunter's vehicle? Shouldn't we take it?"

"No. I've checked it out. They are using hidden locater-devices now. Not enough time to search for them."

"We should destroy it."

Lotar shook his head. "It would bring the Enforcers only sooner."

Renha looked at me. "Can you ride a horse?"

I smiled. "I don't know. Never sat on one."

"Well, you'll have to learn fast. It is either that or walking. Go, help Trembor."

I approached the animal cautiously. I hadn't realized horses were that big. The horse's flanks trembled when I reached out to take off the wrapped bundle it carried on its broad rump.

"She's a mare," Trembor said. "Very gentle for her kind. Don't mistreat her."

"I won't." I carried the heavy bundle to the boat, handed it to one of the men inside.

When the loaded airboat soared into the sky, I was not sorry to see it go. The last thing I needed was quarreling with a bunch of freedom fighters. I climbed onto my steed, made myself comfortable on the thick blanket strapped across its broad back.

Renha already waited impatiently. She sat on her mount as if she belonged there. On her back she carried a backpack and a quiver filled with arrows. The bow she held in one hand, the other hand gripped the reins of her horse.

The horses moved with an easy gait. It didn't take me long to fall into the rhythm. I slipped my boots into loops that were attached to a wide leather band strapped around the belly of the horse. It helped to keep me from losing my balance.

"We're about two days ride away from the outskirts of Tamarok," Renha said, "but it may take longer, because we have to follow the edge of the forest. We're too vulnerable in the open."

"Are you worried about being attacked from the sky?" I asked.

"Seen, mostly. They have eyes in space."

"You mean spy-satellites?"

She nodded. "They think we don't know about them."

I studied her from the side, as she rode beside me. "You seem well educated," I said.

She threw me a scornful look. "You talk like all humans. I am no less intelligent than a human woman...or man."

"I didn't mean to insult you. But considering your species' status on this planet, I am wondering how you manage to be so well informed."

She sighed. "The humans do educate their slaves and servants. Some of us escape and take the knowledge back to the people." She looked at me. "I'm not sure if I should tell you any of this, but I believe I can trust you. Even though my people are considered wild and primitive, we are much further advanced than the humans know. We have computers and a superior communication system. The frequencies we use are so far removed from what the humans use, they will never tap into our communications, but we can monitor theirs."

"What about traveling from place to place? Using horses seems a little primitive to me."

"Why? They are easily available, easy to maintain and arouse no suspicion."

"Where do these horses come from?"

Shrugging, she said, "They have always been here. I think the humans brought them when they came to Eden's Gate. Now they roam free on the Great Plains and in the mountains. The mountain horses are smaller and more agile, also harder to catch."

"I suppose you have better weapons than just bows and arrows."

She chuckled. "You suppose correctly, but the humans must never suspect it."

"*I* know it now, and I am a human."

She gave me a long look, her slit eyes hidden behind long thick lashes. "Are you?" she asked, still looking at me. "We have legends and prophecies," she added, after a long pause.

"Meaning?"

"A stranger will come from the stars. A god in the shape of a man. He will mate with a young female who will bear his son. The son will grow up to be a warlord and he will lead the People in a terrible war against the humans…from which the People will emerge the victors. Eden's Gate will once again belong to its rightful owners."

It was my turn to chuckle. "And you think I am that mysterious stranger?"

"Aren't you?"

"I am a man, not a god, Renha. If I were a god, I would not be sitting on this damn horse and getting a sore ass. I'd fly to Tamarok on my golden wings."

"The ways of the gods have always been strange and mysterious. Who can understand them."

"You're a romantic dreamer, girl. I don't even try to understand *your* ways, never mind the ways of the gods."

We had been following the winding course of a river and ended up at the shore of a small lake. "We'll take a rest," Renha said. "The horses need watering and I could use some food."

"I won't argue with that." Gratefully, I climbed down from the horse, winced when my stiff legs and back protested.

A god indeed!

Chapter Twenty-two

The lake looked peaceful and quiet, and the small, sandy beach seemed like a good place to relax.

A large animal that had been slaking its thirst took flight when we approached, disappearing into the forest. Renha threw her backpack into the white sand, and then she led the horses to the water. "I'm going to take a dip," she announced and looked back at me. "I think it wouldn't do you any harm, either."

I watched her bodysuit pool around her ankles, watched her step out of it. Naked, she stretched, wiggled her lower body. In the light of day she looked even more beautiful. I also realized that she was still quite young, but with the fully developed body of a woman. Her short tail rested inside the deep cleft between her full, round buttocks.

She ran toward the water on long, slender legs, dove headfirst into it. Splashing and laughing she rose up, water dropping from her rows of breasts. "Come, join me. The water is refreshing," she called.

"In other words: cold." I laughed and began stripping off my clothing.

It did feel good.

Renha dove away. I chased her, caught up with her and clamped my hands around her hips. She wriggled in my grasp. Laughing, she turned around and pressed her breasts against my chest. Her hand snaked between us. I felt her warm long fingers curl around my penis. I kissed her hard, probed the insides of her mouth with my tongue. Between my legs, I could feel my penis rise.

She broke the kiss, slipped out of my embrace. Lying on her back, she braced her feet against my thighs and pushed herself away from me. I had a glimpse of her dark thick triangle, and then she disappeared under the water.

"You're a tease," I called after her, but she didn't hear me.

Laughing and blowing water she appeared again, quite a distance away.

"You are a tease," I repeated.

She giggled and shook her breasts. "And you are very impatient," she called back.

She began to wash her hair, rubbed down her body with her hands. She knew I was watching. Once in awhile she threw impish glances in my direction. The she came walking toward me, very slowly. Her upper two breasts jiggled softly. Even though she was very slim, I knew by the rippling of her muscles that she was quite strong.

"Want me to wash you?" she asked. Her slit pupils reflected the light from the overhead sun.

"Go ahead."

She ran her hands down my body; they lingered on my shoulders, on my chest. I felt her long fingers digging into my biceps.

"You must be very strong," she murmured.

When she stood in front of me, I pulled her to me. Grabbing her buttocks, I lifted her up. Her legs parted, wrapped around my body. She was ready for me. Gasping, she impaled herself on my stiff pole. Her sheath felt tight, but creamy enough to let me slide in easily.

I walked with her toward dry land, but she moved so violently that I lost my balance and fell forward. I let go of her buttocks so I could use my hands to keep from crushing her under my weight. Clinging to me, she never stopped moving her hips, and she never lost her tight grip on my penis.

Half submerged in the water, she rested her back on the soft sand, hammering her lower body up against mine.

"Fill me up, now!" she cried into my ear, whimpered loudly as a powerful orgasm gripped her. I pushed deep into her and let go. My discharge jetted into her sucking sex-organ while my own body shook with a tremendous climax. Satiated, I pulled out, lay beside her in the shallow water, breathing deeply.

"You are a great lover," she said after awhile, still gasping for air. "And your seed comes out of you with the force of a waterspout." She turned over onto her stomach, lay half on top of me. Then she kissed me gently. "You know," she whispered, looking into my eyes. "The prophecy has been fulfilled. Your seed and mine will create life inside my womb, and we will have a son."

"Don't talk foolishly. There are ways to prevent fertilization. You are an intelligent girl, I'm sure you are taking precautions."

"I don't. None of our females do. We have to keep multiplying; it is important to our survival."

"You mean every time one of your females copulates she gets pregnant, if she isn't already?"

She laughed, shook her black curls, spraying droplets of water into my face. "No, only when she is in her receptive cycle. I am at the height of my cycle right now."

I sat up, pushed her away, taking care not to hurt her. "You are kidding, of course."

She fell onto her back, lay there looking up at me out of large eyes. "I have never been more serious, Thomas Stone from the stars. I knew the moment I saw you standing there, surrounded by dead Ghouls, that you and I would have a child together. I saw the *God-fire* burning in your eyes."

"It was only the reflection of light. You saw what you wanted to see." I stood up, looked down at her as she lay there on her back, her legs bent at the knees, slightly apart. A young, very beautiful and vulnerable alien girl.

She lifted her arms to me and smiled. "Come, love me again," she said. "And let's not hurry this time."

I fell to my knees between her opening thighs. She reached out, touched my penis with gentle fingers. Very slowly she pulled me toward her. Again her breath caught in her throat when my thick, hard flesh entered her tight sheath. She watched with bright eyes as my pole disappeared inside her belly.

When I was fully lodged inside her, she sighed and searched my face with her purple eyes. "Do you have any other children?" she asked me.

I shook my head. "No. Have you?"

"No."

"Why not? Didn't you tell me you kind breed freely?"

"I was chosen by the gods to bear your son," she said simply.

Foolish girl, I thought, but what did it really matter to me if she suffered from this grand delusion. She was young and hot-blooded, willing and eager to please me. How often is a man this lucky?

I put my hands under her small buttocks, began to move more forcefully between her clutching thighs. Her inner muscles milked me gently; her pelvis gyrated slowly beneath me.

She climaxed several times before I needed to release my own pressure. I saw no more reason to be careful, since I had left my seeds inside her a few times already. If she really did get pregnant, she wanted it.

I began to pump harder. Every thrust moved us closer to dry land. She cried out as another powerful orgasm built up inside her. I felt her shake, go stiff. Digging my fingers into her quivering buttocks, I drove my pulsing rod deep into her creamy sheath and erupted with great force. My climax lasted for a long time, and I held her until I finished.

Her soft cries of pleasure blended with my hoarse shouts.

Neither of us spoke, as we lay clasped in each other's arm, still joined together. After ejaculation, my penis is still rigid for a while. Most women are pleasantly surprised by this fact and usually they will take advantage of the opportunity it presents.

As Renha did. She wriggled her hips and tightened her sheath around my shaft. I rolled over onto my back. She sat up, began to rotate her pelvis in my lap.

"You are a god," she gasped. "No mortal man is capable of keeping it up this long, especially not after releasing his seed."

I took pleasure in seeing her two rows of breasts rippling on her ribcage as she undulated above me, her slim body slick with perspiration and water droplets. She managed to get another orgasm before she collapsed into my arms.

"How can I ever copulate with another male after this?" she said dreamily. "I may have to give it up altogether."

"I don't think that is going to happen." I grinned. "You love it too much."

She sat up. "I'm starving. Let's eat something." She took another dive into the water. I was sitting cross-legged in the sand, watched her as she came back out, hips swinging slightly, rivulets of water running down her tall, lithe body. Standing wide-legged in front of me, she said, "You are looking at me all this time, is something wrong?"

I smiled. "Nothing is wrong. It's just that you look so lovely and innocent. I love looking at you. Beautiful women are my weakness; I can never get enough of them."

"And here I thought you loved only me," she teased. "Come, let's eat."

Without bothering to get dressed, she searched through her backpack, produced a wrapped package and opened it. Then she gave me another one of those brown baked rolls. The water from the plastic bottle taste warm and stale.

It tempted me to drink from the lake, but when I mentioned it, Renha shook her head. "It would make you sick, too many animals bathe in it. Maybe we'll come across a fresh stream later."

After eating I stretched out in the tall grass and lay there, naked, staring into the sky. A few small white clouds were scattered across the blue expanse, but otherwise the sky was clear. The rays of the sun were warm on my skin, I felt comfortable and relaxed. My mind began to wander.

* * * *

Even as children, they were stronger and smarter than the others. They were different. Rumor had it their father was a god. They were not brothers, just cousins, born of two different mothers on the same day; but they could have been brothers, because one looked like the other.

When they were grown they both showed great leadership, and their charismatic personality soon made them leaders in the community. They talked of freedom for the People, freed from the yoke of their human masters.

In secrecy, they built an army, and when they launched their attack, it took the humans by surprise.

Hordes of armed well-trained warriors swarmed into the human cities, killing the sleeping enemy with swift efficiency.

Flying one-man shields rose into the air like swarms of angry insects, descended upon the high-rise buildings, dropping explosives into airshafts, elevators.

Others, who pretended to be loyal servants of the humans, destroyed computer terminals, control towers, and power plants. Then they began to assassinate government officials.

When Planetary Control finally retaliated, millions of human lives had been lost, but now the human military machine began systematically to eliminate the towns and known dwellings of the People.

Fire rained from the sky for days. Yet even with their sophisticated weaponry, the humans could not win the war. The people of the Katre race lived in the mountains, in underground caverns, in the jungle; many lived among the humans.

The humans did not succeed in killing the two leaders of the People. They and a select handful of their key-people managed to capture a small spacecraft. They filled it full of nuclear bombs and took it into space. Their destination was the space station, which housed the military leaders of the planet.

A second sun lit up the night-sky over Eden's Gate, marking the end of human rule.

The Katre took control of all government installations. The People were free at last, but at a great cost.

Years of anarchy followed. The humans did not recognize a

118

Katre government and the Katre would not allow the humans to form their own government. Outside help never came. No other planet would get involved in the affairs of another planet.

Export of drugs and spices ceased to exist, because nobody worked the fields or tended the crops. Pirates took advantage of the undefended position of Eden's Gate and raids were a daily occurrence.

Amidst this chaos, the giant face of a winged, golden man covered the sky. He smiled, and then laughed.

* * * *

The thunder of his laughter woke me up.

I shuddered and sat up. Above me, the sky was bright and blue.

Chapter Twenty-three

We arrived at *Bent Grass* before nightfall. Nestled along the banks of a winding river it could have been any village on any planet settled by humans. The houses were small, with low, thatched roofs. The doors hung on hinges and the windowpanes were made out of glass.

When we rode down the main road, we received curious glances from the people we met. All of them had Renha's eyes, and I knew they were not human.

Renha, too, saw those glances. "They are wondering what I am doing in the company of a Hunter. You are wearing a Hunter's coat."

"They don't seem to be afraid."

"They have no reason to be. As long as they are inside the village boundaries they are safe."

"There are humans living in this village?"

"The only humans are the Overseers and the guards in the tower."

"Where are we going?"

"I have friends here. They will give us shelter and food."

I shifted the backpack I had offered to carry for her from one shoulder to the other. "This thing is beginning to get heavy," I said. "I could use some rest."

It was a lie. I hardly get tired, and when I do, I need very little rest to recuperate. However, I knew she was close to exhaustion. She was a strong girl, but not like Sharina and Kabrina, who seemed to have no need for rest at all. I wondered what they were up to right now. Too bad I lost my communicator.

"What are the people here doing for a living?" I asked Renha.

"They fish in the river, but most of them work in the fields," she said.

"They grow food?"

"Not food. Spices and herbs."

"Which they sell to the humans."

Renha laughed bitterly. "Not sell. The humans come and take them. This land belongs to the humans. Katre do not own property."

"What about food?"

"They are allowed to grow vegetables in designated gardens. Also, there are plenty of edible creatures in the river." She reigned in before one of the houses. "My friend lives here."

I dismounted, stiff-legged and sore. It felt good to have soil beneath my soles.

The door into the house opened and a young Katre-woman, wearing a loose-fitting robe made from coarse fibers, stepped out, a little older than Renha, but not much. When she saw me, her eyes narrowed. I could read the hostility in her face. Then she looked at Renha, puzzled.

Renha smiled thinly. "He is not what he seems. He's an off-worlder who got himself lost."

"A *human* off-worlder," the other girl said.

"He's a friend." Renha looked at me and smiled. "More than a friend, much more."

"He wears a Hunter's coat."

"The coat of a dead Hunter. It is a long story. Aren't you going to invite us in?"

"You shouldn't come here. It is dangerous."

"I live with danger every day, my dear cousin. Go, get Sarr to look after the horses. I am too tired." Renha grabbed my arm. "Come, Thomas, Rinca may seem hostile, but she is really a sweet girl. Once she'll get to know you she will love you, too."

She pulled me into the house, past the girl, who still wasn't quite sure about me. I didn't know what to expect inside the house, but the cleanliness surprised me. The room was not large, the furniture simple, but functional. Off to one side I saw a small nook with a woodstove that provided warmth for cool nights and also served as a means to cook food.

Two curtain-covered doors in one wall led into, what I assumed, bedrooms.

"You can sleep in there." Rinca pointed to one of the doors. She walked ahead of us, pulled the curtain aside.

I stepped past her, was happy to see a real bed, nice and wide, too. I threw Renha's backpack onto the bed and turned toward the girl. "My name is Thomas Stone," I introduced myself. "Like Renha said, I am her friend and hope to become yours, also."

She gave me a hesitant smile. "We'll see."

I liked her. She looked as beautiful as Renha, especially when she smiled. The resemblance was almost uncanny. They could have been sisters. She wore her hair longer than Renha's, black and curly, tied with a ribbon behind her head.

"I assume you are hungry," she said, lowered her lashes when she became aware that I studied her.

"You are as beautiful as your cousin," I told her. She smiled, but said nothing.

Renha rested on a cloth-covered wide bench, her eyes half-closed. "I could go to sleep right now," she said as we came into the room.

"When did you eat last?" Rinca asked her.

"I don't remember," Renha murmured. "A long time ago."

When Rinca looked at me, I chuckled. "We ate at noon, but it wasn't much. I could use some food."

"What about the horses?" Renha asked sleepily.

"I'll get Sarr," Rinca said and walked out of the door.

"Who's Sarr?" I asked Renha.

"He's a cousin, Rinca's brother. He lives with his family in the house next to this one."

Rinca came back a short time later and began to search for food in her cupboard. "I don't have much," she apologized. "Just some bread and cheese, dried meat, one smoked fish, and Swark-milk."

"Forget the Swark-milk," I said, remembering the first time I drank it. "Water would be welcome."

Rinca laughed, and with a glance at Renha, she said, "So you've tasted it. Most humans don't care for it."

Renha smirked. "He's tasted Swark-milk and other things, too. He liked both."

"Would it offend you if I took off this coat?" I asked Rinca.

She shook her head. "It offends me to see you wear the coat. It awakens painful memories."

"Her father was killed by a Hunter," Renha explained.

I took off the coat, rolled it into a ball. "Get rid of it, then," I said.

There was a strange expression on Rinca's face when she looked at my naked torso. "You are very muscular," she said. "Most human males I've seen have flabby bodies."

"Surely there are some Katre-men who are muscular."

"Muscular, yes, but not like you."

"Does the sight of my body revolt you?"

"No." The flickering light from the oil lamp that hung from the ceiling reflected in her purple eyes as she studied me. "I find you…intriguing." She exchanged glances with Renha, but neither girl said anything to the other.

I did have some Swark-milk, felt the effect almost immediately. Both girls drank more than they should have, and I couldn't miss the looks Rinca threw at the bulge in my pants.

After eating, I leaned back in my chair, made myself as comfortable as possible. The seat was padded with some soft material, but the back was straight and hard. "You don't have electricity," I remarked.

"We are not allowed such luxuries," Rinca said. "The humans prefer us to live in primitive conditions." She smiled without humor. "Our wild cousins live in more modern surroundings than we do, even though they are supposed to be the uneducated savages."

"Your house is very clean."

"We are not animals." Rinca wiped the table with a coarse cloth, and then washed the cloth in a small basin filled with water, which she emptied into a basin sunk into the countertop of a small cabinet beside the stove. I heard the water rushing down a pipe.

"You have indoor plumbing," I said.

Rinca blew a puff of air through her nose. "My father built this house. He was a smart man, and a dreamer. He should have left this place a long time ago and joined the wild bands. He'd be alive today."

"What about your mother?"

She shrugged. "The Hunters who killed my father captured her and sold her to some rich House."

"She may have a better life than you."

"She is a slave. I belong to no-one!"

"I don't understand this whole thing with the Hunters. Why are they allowed to hunt your people?"

"We are nothing but animals to the humans. As long as we stay in our assigned place, we are safe. Anywhere else, we are meat. This is how it has always been. We have to accept that."

"But not all of us do." Renha, who had been following our conversation with mild interest, injected savagely. "Some of them will never hunt again."

"I'm afraid to ask what you mean," Rinca said, "but I can imagine. If you are found here, you will be returned to the House you escaped from. They'll make sure you never escape again."

"I will not be captured again!" Renha took another swig of Swark-milk, burped loudly. "I don't know about you, but I am going to bed."

"So am I," Rinca said. "I have to get up early in the morning."

123

She looked at me. "Renha can sleep with me tonight. You are a big man; you need more room than Renha or I."

I got up. "Where are your facilities?" I asked.

"Our facilities?" Rinca chuckled. "They are in the back, but don't expect anything fancy." She went to the cupboard, brought out a small oil-lamp, and lit it with the flame from a torch. "Here," she said. "It is dark outside."

I had no trouble finding what I was looking for. I guess an outhouse is an outhouse on any planet where humans live. As Rinca had said, nothing fancy, but the small basin with a drain surprised me. A plastic pipe with a valve at the end provided running water.

I washed my hands, dried them on my pants, and then I headed back toward the house. Before I went back in, I looked around in the darkness. Eden's Gate does have any satellites to provide illumination at night.

To the east I could see the bright top of a giant mushroom, the lights of Tamarok. It didn't seem that far away. A few circles of blinking lights moved across the night-sky, entering the bright dome of light. Most of them came from the south, probably another city. Closer by, at the end of the village, a small bright spot: the guard-tower.

It was getting chilly. The nights do get cool in this part of the planet. I went inside the house. Quietly I entered my room and found the bed already occupied, so I shut off the oil supply to my lamp, watched the little flame die. Naked, I slipped under the covers. The mattress felt comfortable enough, and I stretched out with a feeling of satisfaction.

I didn't know how long I had slept when the touch of a warm hand on my chest aroused me. "Are you asleep?" a voice whispered.

"Not anymore," I whispered back.

"Good." She slid on top of me. A row of soft breasts flattened against my chest and belly. "You can sleep later," she whispered and snaked her hand down to my groin. Warm, long fingers curled around my already reacting penis. Then she took my pole between her soft, strong thighs. Slowly she rubbed her slit over the hard knob. It didn't take long until I felt warm liquid running down the insides of my buttocks. With a little cry, she lifted her hips and impaled herself deeply on my hard rod.

Her inner muscles tightened and a soft vice slid up and down on my shaft with ferocious speed. She climaxed several times, let out a long wailing cry each time she doused me with her hot fluid.

I let her play as long as she wanted. When her movements slowed, I put her onto her back. Her knees bent sharply as she opened her legs wide, and now it was my turn to move fast and furious. Her pelvis churned underneath me and her hips hammered up against mine.

"Now!" she exclaimed with a loud whisper, "come inside me now, before I faint from exhaustion."

With a grunt I relaxed, held her tight as my spermatic fluid shot into her womb. My climax lasted for a long time. With each spurt it seemed to reach a higher level.

She became limp in my arms when I finally finished, her breath came in loud gasps.

"You surely are a god. No mortal man can achieve this."

She kissed me briefly on the mouth and whispered, "I'm going to sleep with my cousin. Otherwise neither one of us is going to get any rest tonight."

I closed my eyes, heard her slip from the bed and pad on soft soles out of the door.

I awoke at dawn. Opening my eyes, I saw the shadowy figure of a slim, naked Katre-girl outlined against the curtain. Moving silently, she came to my bed, lifted the covers, then she stretched out beside me and pressed her warm, soft body against mine.

"I missed you inside me last night," she purred and touched my penis.

"What do you mean, you missed me...who did I...?" I stopped and chuckled.

That sly, little devil! I should have known. Each woman moves and feels a little different; even two look-alike cousins will not behave the same. It must have been the Swark-milk that befuddled my brain.

"Rinca is still sleeping. She seems really exhausted. She works too hard."

"I bet she does." I grinned and rolled on top of Renha. I found her ready and willing. Her thighs flew open and took me deep into her. Gasping, she moved against me, began milking me with savage thrusts of her pelvis.

"We don't have much time," she moaned. "Rinca will rise soon." She came with a keening wail, sobbed loudly into my ear.

"You sound just like your cousin when you come," I said, and pinned her to the mattress.

"I don't know what you mean." Her long fingers raked down my back, dug into my buttocks.

"She spent half the night in my bed," I told her. "And don't tell me that you don't know. She made enough noise to wake the dead."

Renha smiled, sighed deeply and pulled me down. She held me tight against her soft breasts. She lay still, only her inner walls were pulsing around my penis. "I wanted her to feel the rod of a god inside her. I wanted her to drink the gift of a god. I never told you the whole prophecy. It speaks of two warrior-lords who will be born to two young maidens. They will be half-brothers, because they have only one father; yet, they will not know this."

"That is just great! I suppose your cousin is also at the peak of her cycle right now?"

"She is, just like me." Renha gasped, slammed her hips up against mine. I felt her hot discharge, pushed deep into her, and with each throb of my member, I shot a jet of my own fluid into her welcoming womb. She sucked it up with joy, clamped her long legs around me until I was finished.

I rolled away from her, lay beside her on my back.

"Are you angry?" she asked after her breathing became normal again.

I turned my head to look into her large questing eyes. "No," I said, "just curious why you would want a man, who you will never see again, father your child. Why would you want to raise a son who will not know his father?"

She smiled. "I told you. And you need not worry. Your sons will not lack love and they will be raised by the Katre-people, not by humans."

I sensed movement by the door. The curtain was pushed aside and Rinca walked through, naked and lovely looking, and smiling. "I heard everything," she said. "I'd like to apologize for deceiving you, but we were afraid you may not want to couple with me."

"To deny a beautiful girl like you?" I answered. "I wouldn't be such a fool."

She jumped on top of the bed, straddled me, and before I could stop her she pushed herself onto my still hard member. Her sheath felt tight, but hot and slippery, and laughing she snapped her pelvis up and down with the ferocity of a tree-cat. Her slit eyes bored into mine, and when she came, she never took them off my face.

"I want to burn your image into my brain forever, so I can

describe to my son what his father looked like," she said between gaps and sat quivering in my lap until her orgasm had subsided.

She lifted up, let Renha take her place. I studied the two rows of her breasts as she lazily gyrated her hips. Lifting my hands, I stroked them gently. The nipples on her smaller breasts seemed to have increased in size, as well as her breasts.

Rinca bent over me to kiss me. Her tongue snaked into my mouth. She tasted of spices and sweet fruit. Her teeth were sharp, and she sank them teasingly into my tongue. When she released me I pulled Renha down, pressed my lips against hers. She opened her mouth, let my tongue enter. She tasted different, but pleasant. Her teeth were as sharp as those of her cousin.

She pulled away, sat up and laughed down at me. "We only kiss a lover like that," she said and increased the speed of her movements.

Time for me to release my own pressure. When I grabbed her hips, she shook her head, slid off me. She pointed at Rinca who knelt beside us on the bed. I moved into position behind the girl. She pushed up her round buttocks, arched her back. Below her cheeks the puffy lips of her sex-organ were clearly visible. I slid my hard member between her cheeks, felt the soft lips open as I pushed forward. With a grunt, I entered her tight sheath deeply. She began to buck immediately. I grabbed her hips, steadied her and began pumping.

Groaning, I let myself explode inside her. She cried out, her fingers dug into the bedcovers and her inner muscles began milking me until I was dry. Then we both fell forward. My penis was still buried inside her, when I heard a loud pounding at the front door, and then someone broke into the house, shouting with an authoritative voice.

Chapter Twenty-four

They were descent enough to let me put on my pants and boots. The sheath of my combat-knife was built into the boot, but they probably would have missed it anyway. It was not a common weapon. When I slipped into my boots, I turned to avoid the chance a sharp observer might detect the small bulge.

There were three of them. Two with drawn flash-rifles and one with just a scowl on his face and a thin black mustache under a nose a trifle too big. I registered his gun secure in the holster he had strapped to his hip.

"For an off-worlder you speak our language remarkably well, Senjar Stone. If that really is your name."

"I'm sure you, too, have methods were one can learn a foreign language in a few hours. It is no great feat."

"We have, but such devices are expensive and not very reliable. I think you are lying. What a coincidence that you should loose your wallet with your ID. Tell me again how you lost it."

"I told you, I was robbed."

"Oh, right, you were robbed. And how did you end up here, of all places? Don't you know that only authorized personnel are allowed in this area?"

"I was taken out of the city in an aircraft and dropped in the wilderness. These young ladies rescued me."

His scowl became even deeper. "People who can afford an aircraft have no reason to rob other people. By the way, are those your horses outside?"

I shrugged. "I borrowed them. How else could I have gotten here?"

He managed a tight laugh. "Borrowed! I think *you* are the thief here." He stared at me out of gray steely eyes. "You like fucking Katre females?"

"Don't you?" I countered.

One of the guards tried to hit me with the butt of his rifle, but I saw it coming and went with the blow, then I struck the weapon out of his hands. It clattered to the floor with a loud crash. The other guard aimed his rifle at my head.

"You're fast," my interrogator said. "There is more to you than it seems."

"I've had training," I said mildly. "I don't take well to being mistreated, but I should not be surprised, I mean, the way you treat your indigenous people here."

"You are treading on dangerous ground, Senjar."

I looked at the guard who was pushing his weapon into my face. "Can you point that thing somewhere else? It makes me nervous."

"You talk big for a man with a gun to his head," the guard growled.

I could have unarmed this one, too, but I knew there were more outside. "You must have a computer terminal at your station. You can easily confirm my identity; just get in touch with the spaceport authorities." I addressed the man with the scowl, smiled at him. "You never introduced yourself, Senjar."

"I am Overseer Sanchet." His thin mustache twitched. "I am in charge of this whole section. Nothing ever happens here that I will not be made aware of."

"How did you find out about me?" I asked.

"A human rides into a Katre-town on a horse? Come on, Senjar Stone, don't be a fool. It will be reported to me."

"So you've got snitches among the slaves, interesting."

"They are not snitches, just good law-abiding citizens."

"Citizens who have no rights," I sneered.

Suddenly a gun appeared in his hand and only centimeters away from my nose. "One more slanderous remark like that and we won't have to worry about your identity," he snarled.

"Touchy subject, isn't it?" I said, not easily intimidated.

""It is true. We have no rights." I turned my head slowly to look at Renha who had spoken. She stood naked in the doorway, hands on hips, her two rows of breasts taut on her pushed-out ribcage, a defiant look in her purple eyes.

"Your opinion has not been asked for, Katre-female. Get back into your room until I call you!" Overseer Sanchet spoke sharply, his voice full of contempt and disgust.

When Renha turned around, she exposed her left shoulder, displaying her blue tattoo.

"Hold it!" Sanchet snapped. "That mark! It is the sign of the *House of Bluestone*. You are an escaped slave."

"She's anyone's property now," one of the guards said. "What about it, Overseer?"

Sanchet stood up. "You!" he said to me. "Come with me. We'll find out who you really are." Then he turned to the guards. "I'll give you two hours. I don't care if she is alive or dead when you are through with her. But make sure the other one is alive and ready to go to work."

He didn't know that he had just signed his own death warrant. His head exploded with a loud pop, tiny pieces of his brain sprayed into my face. I didn't need to look at the doorway where Renha stood to know what happened. My knife came out of my boot in an instant, I drew it across the nearest guard's throat, and in the same motion let it fly to sink it to the hilt into the other one's chest.

The small explosion would surely attract the attention of the guards outside. Pulling my knife out of the dead man's chest, I moved to the door, waited for the door to open.

Moments later it opened, a man with a flash-rifle stuck his head inside. I grabbed him, pulled him into the room and slammed the door shut again. He saw the dead bodies, opened his mouth to call out, but I broke his neck with a sharp blow of my balled fist.

If there were any more guards outside I would have to deal with them, too. We couldn't leave any witnesses alive.

"Why did you have to kill the Overseer?" I asked Renha, who was still stood in the doorway, her bow in her hand. "You put us into a precarious situation."

"I told you, I will not live in captivity again. Besides, he ordered me dead, you heard him. They would have sunk their filthy organs into my belly over and over, these two and the others. They would have hurt me, tortured me, and then let me bleed to death." She stared at me. "I am carrying your son, Thomas Stone, he must be born. I had no choice."

"You took quite a chance. The other two guards could have shot you."

She smiled. "I knew you wouldn't let that happen."

Rinca appeared behind her, already dressed. "We must leave," she said to Renha. "You and I. My life here is finished; they will kill me, too."

"I know." Renha nodded. "Our sons will be born free."

"What about me?" I asked.

"We can't accompany you, but I promised to get you to Tamarok and I will keep my promise." Renha disappeared into the bedroom, while her cousin rushed into the other room to pack a few things. At least that is what I assumed.

Time to get dressed. I still had nothing I could use to cover my upper body.

Rinca came out of her room, carrying a backpack.

"You wouldn't have anything I could wear?" I asked her.

She looked me over. "You are a big man," she said, "but I still have an old coat which belonged to my father. It was always too large for him, but it might fit you." She went back into the room, came back a few moments later, carrying a coat. I slipped into it, found it tight around my shoulders, but it would have to do.

Renha joined us. She carried her bow in her hand, her backpack slung across her shoulder.

"There may still be guards waiting outside," I cautioned.

"We'll have to kill them, too," Renha said, matter-of-factly. "No-one must see us leave."

She was right, of course.

"It has to be done in here, no witnesses. By the time they find the bodies we should be far away," I said.

"I'll go outside, find them and lure them back in here." Rinca put her pack on the counter in the kitchen nook. She looked at the four dead bodies on the floor. "It is getting crowded in here. We should move them."

I pulled the bodies into one of the bedrooms, piled them on top of the bed. They were still bleeding, blood soaked into the bed coverings, staining them red. It didn't matter; Rinca would have no more use for them.

"What about all the blood on the floor?" Rinca asked when I got back into the living room. I shook my head. "Anyone coming in here will be dead before he sees it."

She opened the door carefully and walked out. I took my place beside it, waited. It didn't take long until I heard someone knock on the door. "I'm coming back in," Rinca called. "Alone." She rushed in, closed the door behind her. "There is nobody there. Sarr is getting the horses ready for us. I told him what happened. Let's hurry."

The horses were saddled and waiting for us when we got outside. Rinca's brother, Sarr, greeted us with a grim expression on his face. He was tall and slim, like his sister and his cousin. A little older than Rinca. I noticed his callused hands.

"So, you are the mysterious stranger from the stars," he said, scowling. "I wish you wouldn't have come. My sister would not have to leave now."

"I'm sorry you feel that way. It was not my decision to come here."

"It doesn't matter, it has happened. You must all leave before more damage is done." He looked at his sister, clasped her hands. "Promise me, never to return here, not even to visit. You'll be killed on sight."

She pulled his hands away, put her arms around his neck. "Stay safe, brother."

Then she swung herself onto one of the horses. Renha mounted the other one, told me to get onto Rinca's horse.

"Give me a hand," I said to Sarr. "I am not used to riding these beasts." I stepped into his locked hands and managed to join Rinca on the animal's broad rump. I had barely time to put my arms around the girl's chest when the horse took off. In my hands her breasts felt soft and pliable, and I was careful not to squeeze them too hard as I hung on, trying not to fall off. Because of the backpack, I sat far back in an uncomfortable position and I had no stirrups to balance myself.

We galloped down the narrow street, away from the guard-tower. Fortunately, there was no one on the street. The fewer people that saw us leave, the safer we would be.

We turned into a side road that led toward the river. I saw a small harbor, with a few vessels moored to the dock. The stench of fish-guts, oil, and seaweed clung strongly to the crisp morning air, and the shrill cry of seabirds disturbed the peaceful silence.

The horse's hoofs clattered on the thick weather-beaten timbers as we galloped toward one of the larger ships. Sailors hoisted a huge sail. I saw a couple of men walking on deck, another one on the dock, untying a thick rope.

The man with the rope looked up as we raced toward him. Renha's horse reared up when she pulled sharply on the reins. She slid off and approached the man. She spoke to him with an urgent voice, pointing at me. He looked up, nodded slowly.

"This is as far as I can go with you," Renha said to me as she mounted her horse again. "You can trust Sarros, he is a good friend. He will take you to Tamarok."

"How?"

"On his ship. He is a fisherman and he has legitimate reasons to go there."

I jumped off the horse, stepped up to Renha. "Thank you for

helping me, a complete stranger and a human. I'm sorry I put you and your cousin into this predicament."

She smiled, bent down to kiss me. Her lips were hot on mine. I hated to break our kiss. "None of us had a choice in the matter. It was pre-destined." Touching my cheek, she said, "We will take good care of your sons. Go now."

I turned without looking back, walked toward the man watching me. He was big, larger and bulkier than any Katre-male I had met so far. Corded muscles covered his naked upper torso. He had well-developed pectoral muscles, but the three nipples below them were just small, thick black dots. Too much exposure to the sun had tanned his skin and left deep cracks on his face.

"I am Sarros," he said. "I will take you to the City."

I nodded, stepped onto the narrow plank that joined the ship to land. He came right behind me. I helped him pull the plank onto the ship.

"Go below deck," he told me. "Away from curious eyes."

Before I climbed down the hatchway I looked toward the dock, but the girls were already galloping away.

Chapter Twenty Five

The river wound its way toward Tamarok like a giant snake, twisting this way and that through a landscape dotted with small forests and cultivated fields. To reach the city would have been faster on land, but I didn't have much choice in the manner of transportation. The journey would take at least three days, mainly because on our way there we'd have to stop several times to do some fishing.

Altogether, there were eight people on board. Two of the sailors were manning the sails and one stood at the wheel that controlled the rudder. That left five to do the rest of the chores, like scrubbing the deck, cooking and throwing out the nets. I made myself as useful as possible. Because I didn't know anything about fishing and sailing, Captain Sarros appointed me *First Scrubber*. I had no idea that my knees could get so sore, not to mention my back.

The sails were never quite full, since we seldom got strong winds, and the current was quite weak. Traveling would definitely have been speedier on horseback.

The river was wide; in my estimation roughly a couple of kilometers. There were other vessels on the water, sailing in either direction, most of them smaller than ours, and faster.

The first impression one got from Captain Sarros was that of a rough, non-communicative character, but he turned out to be quite amiable and talkative.

In the evening we sat in the common mess hall and talked by the dim light of oil-lamps hanging from the ceiling. *Mess hall* was maybe the wrong word for this narrow, low-ceilinged, cramped stinking dungeon; but it felt good to sit after spending most of the day on my knees, scrubbing rough planks that had no chance of ever becoming clean.

We ate from plastic plates and drank cheap wine out of plastic beakers. The fare was simple and predictable: boiled tubers and freshly caught fish.

All of the men smoked pipes after supper; the sweet aroma of the crushed leaves of some mild drug was actually not unpleasant, but I was not used to breathing smoke-laden air and therefore I spent half my night coughing my lungs out. The men thought it was quite amusing, and I suspect they smoked more than they usually would have.

"You know, you should feel privileged, Thomas Stone," Captain Sarros said, puffing rings of smoke.

"Why is that?" I asked, trying hard to ignore the tickling in my throat.

"Because you are the first human ever to sit in the bowels of this ship, the first human to share a meal with us."

I lost the battle with my throat and exploded noisily. One of the men beside me clapped me on the back under the sympathetic laughter of the others.

"I have a spare pipe I could lend you, Thomas," the Captain said. "Maybe if you'd smoke you might be able to breathe easier."

"No, thanks." I waived him off. "Some fresh air on deck may be more beneficial."

"I wouldn't advise going on deck," the man beside me said. "The night brings out the *Nightflyers*. Fresh human meat is a delicacy."

"That doesn't surprise me. I was under the impression that Eden's Gate was a paradise, but I am inclined to change that assumption. So far Eden's Gate has been nothing but Hell for me," I said.

Captain Sarros laughed good-humoredly. "That's why this world is called Eden's *Gate*. Paradise is on the other side." He bent across the table, peered at me through the smoke. "Tell me about other worlds."

"What do you want to know?"

"Are they like this one? Do humans hate non-humans on every world?"

"Each world is different. Some are like yours, some are hot and humid, others cold and harsh. Some worlds are covered mostly by water, some are dry and dusty, and water is a highly prized commodity. Humans adapt to all kinds of environments, but one thing never changes, their hatred of what is different. Humans will enslave, even kill, their own brothers if their eyes are of a different shape or their skin a different color."

"Why?"

I shrugged. "If it makes you feel any better, humans do not have the monopoly when it comes to discrimination. There are actually worlds out there where humans are the under-trodden and kept as slaves."

"That may be so, but it changes nothing for us."

I looked around the smoke-filled room. I couldn't make up my mind if the smoke was worse than the rancid smell of the oil from the lamps or the overpowering stink from the fish. "You seem to live not too badly," I said. "You have your ship, you are free."

There was choked laughter from Captain Sarros and his crew.

"You are either mocking us or you are really that ignorant." The Captain showed strong, sharp teeth. "We may look like savages, and it may seem that we like living in these cramped, stinking conditions. Agreed, it is better than working in the fields, and we do have a certain freedom, but we know how the humans live in their fancy towers in the cities." His fist slammed down on the table. "And this ship, it does not belong to me. We Katre do not own anything, not even our lives."

"Who owns the ship?"

"The same humans who own the river and all the fish in it. We are not free, Thomas Stone. My crew and I can never leave this ship. Every day and night we sail this river, catching as many fish as we can. We take our catch to Tamarok, and then we come back again."

"I was told that the so-called wild Katre live under better conditions. You could just leave and join your people in the mountains or in the forest."

He leaned back, gave me a wolfish grin. "I could," he said, "but who would keep an eye on the Humans?" He stretched and yawned. "It is time to get some sleep."

I felt ready myself to give these weary bones their deserved rest. "Where can I sleep?" I asked.

He smiled. "You are probably used to fancier quarters, so I must apologize for our humble facilities."

Humble was correct.

I shared my sleeping quarters with a thousand pounds of smelly fish cadavers.

"It is a bit chilly in there," said the man who showed me my little suit, grinning broadly, and handed me an equally smelly blanket.

Finding myself inside a refrigerator, certainly surprised me. The gentle humming of an air-conditioning unit, powered by a small energy-cell, was almost soothing. A light-strip built into the ceiling provided illumination.

Strange to see such modern equipment among these primitive surroundings.

The refrigeration unit kept the temperature just above freezing. Too damn cold. I shivered inside my blanket, but I did manage to fall asleep. I dreamt again.

* * * *

The golden man hovered above me. "You did this to yourself, you know that, don't you?"

Before I could answer, my perception shifted. He didn't hover above me, but above another man. A man with golden skin, and velvety, black wings.

"I know I did," said the black-winged one. "But that was a long time ago."

"Time is meaningless to the Guardians."

"Do they ever forgive?"

"They don't carry grudges."

"I did nothing wrong."

"There is no such thing as right or wrong. As I told you before, it is a matter of balance. Order or chaos."

The black-winged one rose to his feet, his black wings hung like a cloak from his wide shoulders. "Only chaos brings about changes and progress, peace is the end of everything."

"Chaos also brings turmoil, hatred, greed and lust," the golden man said gently. "Peace is Love."

"Peace is Death."

The golden man shook his head, spread his hands. "Your banishment will come to an end soon," he predicted. "It must be so. Nothing goes on forever. What begins will end."

"And begin again."

A frown crossed the golden forehead. "Throughout eternity," he whispered. "Nothing ever changes."

He looked down at me. My perception shifted again. When I looked around, I couldn't see the one with black wings.

"Nothing ever changes," the golden man said again. He began to beat his wings furiously, shooting into the darkening sky.

Snow began to fall. The air became cold, freezing. I felt cold.

* * * *

I awoke and looked around in the darkness, drew the blanket tighter around my shivering body.

Why was I so obsessed with that golden man?

Chapter Twenty-six

"Hey, First Scrubber, give us a hand here."

I dropped my mob and rushed to help the men pull up the heavy net. Fish flopped on my freshly scrubbed deck, but I didn't care. So I'd scrub it again. It was my job. I wouldn't want to do this for the rest of my life, though.

"I think you're bringing us luck, Thomas Stone." Captain Sarros stepped over the flopping fish, beaming. "We haven't had a catch like this for a long time."

"Well, I'm glad I can bring somebody luck."

The sails were hanging slack because of the lack of wind, so the two men, who usually manned the sails, helped us gut the fish. Once they were gutted and cleaned, we put them into large basket, then we carried them below deck into the coolers.

My sleeping quarters would be a bit more cramped tonight.

Captain Sarros slapped me on the shoulder. "Come, share a beaker of wine with me."

It was close to suppertime and the end of the day. The other men began cleaning themselves up. I followed the captain down into his cabin, a small, cramped place, but still more comfortable than the quarters of the crew.

"You never told me what exactly it is you're doing on our planet." He seated himself behind a small desk and began to light his pipe, then he put it aside with a little smile. I felt grateful for that. The stink of fish was enough for my sensitive nose.

"Business," I said. "We came to do business."

"You're a trader?"

I smiled. "You could call me that. I used to be a soldier."

"Who did you fight?"

"The enemy." I chuckled. "The universe is an ugly place. Conflict isn't hard to find. Nations will fight nations. Planets will make war with other planets. That will never change. A soldier has no problem finding work."

"Then why did you quit?" His cat's eyes watched me with lazy interest.

"I didn't." I took a sip from my beaker. The wine didn't taste any better since I had sampled it for the first time. "I had a slight disagreement with my superiors."

He leaned forward, his eyes flickering in the dim light of the oil lamp. "What is your relationship with Renha?"

"She rescued me and I in turn rescued her. Perhaps some day she'll tell you the story."

He grinned. "She's a wild one. She told me she'd hunt me down if I let anything happen to you. She said you and she were lovers."

"That girl has a fertile imagination," I said. "She told you the truth. We were lovers."

"And her cousin, Rinca?"

"Not lovers, but I shared her bed. Why do you want to know?"

"I want to understand why human males seek out Katre females. Why did you?"

I shrugged. "I didn't seek them out. We met by chance."

He reached for his pipe, took something out of a clay jar, stuffed it into the bowl of his pipe, and lit it with a light-stick. Puffing vigorously, he was soon enveloped by a bluish cloud of smoke.

"Nothing ever happens by chance. You say you're a soldier. Could you teach us to fight?"

"I could. But I don't plan to stay long enough. I'd like to get off this planet as fast as I can." I suppressed an urge to cough.

"Even Renha couldn't persuade you to stay?"

"She never asked me to. I don't think I fit into her plans." I smiled. "I believe I gave her what she wanted."

He broke into sudden laughter. His teeth flashed in his craggy face. "I don't think it was an unfair bargain. Our young females are quite desirable, especially when they give themselves freely."

"Let me ask you a question, Captain Sarros. Are there still descendants of the original Katre people left on this planet?"

He shook his head. "Nobody knows. Although there are rumors that a few wild tribes live in the jungles to the south. But those are only rumors." He took a drag from his pipe, watched the smoke swirl around. "Even if they exist, it wouldn't matter. We, the bastard offspring, are the real inheritors of Eden's Gate. The legends tell us so."

"Legends always seem to exaggerate," I said.

"Maybe." He lifted a finger. "Be silent for a moment and listen. What do you hear?"

"I hear the creaking of old and tired timbers, the cracking of decaying boards. I hear the sounds of a ship."

"That's right. But if you listen closely, you hear more than that.

These boards and those timbers used to be living trees at one time. Their ghosts are still in this ship. The ship talks to us. It tells us the story of the trees and of our people. It tells us the future."

"All I hear is creaking and cracking."

"Because you are not part of this planet. *I am*. I can hear it speaking to me. The stories have changed since you came aboard. The ship speaks of you."

"What does it say?"

He looked at me for a long time. "It speaks of violence, of insurgence, of death. It speaks of changes. Not all of them good. I told you before that you bring us luck, but it is not only luck you bring with you, Thomas Stone. There is that within you which will shake the foundations of the worlds you touch."

"Are you saying I carry evil inside me?" I asked.

"Not evil. Neither is it good." Captain Sarros closed his eyes. He seemed to listen. When he opened them again, he murmured, "Turmoil follows you wherever you go. You sow chaos, Senjar Thomas Stone. Chaos."

Chapter Twenty-seven

We heard the screaming jets of the three Skimmers before they came shooting around the small island that lay ahead of us. The noise was purely for entertainment and excitement. The riders could have chosen to skim the water in complete silence.

I was just helping the crew to pull in one of the nets, heavy with a large catch of fish, when two of the small craft began circling our ship, creating large waves that hindered our efforts to pull the net onto the deck.

"Hey!" yelled one of the crewmen and shook his fist at the riders.

"Be careful." One of the others hissed a warning. "They are *Holy Golden Warriors.*"

The three men wore golden armor. It covered their chest, shoulders, and neck. They had shaved heads, with a long, thin braid hanging down their back. The third rider, who bobbed on the waves in front of us, produced a short rifle and with a sweep of the narrow beam he cut off the top of our net, sending it and its contents into the depth of the river. When the resistance on the ropes we were pulling suddenly vanished, we stumbled backwards and ended in a tangled heap on the slippery deck.

Even above the roar of their revved-up engines could we hear their laughter. The same crewman who shook his fist leaned over the railing and shouted an obscenity at the shooter.

I had just managed to get back on my feet when I saw the rider lift his rifle again and fire it.

The Katre-man let out a gurgled cry and collapsed into a lifeless heap. When I looked at the man who fired the deadly shot he shouted, "You want to be the next, Katre-scum?"

I reached into the inside of my coat pocket and pulled out the small sidearm I had taken from Overseer Sanchet, aimed it at the man on the craft and drilled a hole into his forehead. He didn't even have time to scream.

His buddies watched him collapse. One of them cursed and reached for a rifle, which was strapped to the hood in front of him. I moved my own weapon, but when I pushed the firing stud, nothing happened.

Damn that Sanchet for being so sloppy! I used up the very last charge.

With the rifle aimed at me, I felt the wave of Darkness well up again. Leaping over the railing I dove into the water, my eyes adjusted automatically to the slight murkiness. Under water I swam in the direction of the watercraft, saw the dark shape above me. With my knife already in my hand, I surfaced beside the craft.

Rising above the surface, I reached for his braid, pulled back his head. The blade of my knife gleamed brightly as I slashed it across his throat, slicing the protective armor and the soft flesh beneath, severing his windpipe and artery. Before he slipped into the waves, I pried the rifle from his lifeless fingers, swung onto the sled and looked for the third man.

He stared at me wide-eyed from three meters away, not quite comprehending what just happened. What he saw in my face must have scared the hell out of him.

"Please," he mouthed, lifting one hand. He was young, like the others. Young, reckless, and arrogant.

I could let him live...but then again, there couldn't be any witnesses. He knew it. With a shout, he gunned his engine and tried to ram my craft.

The Darkness raged still inside me. My mind felt cold, merciless. I shot him without regret. He would have done the same to me.

The Katre-men were gathering at the railing, staring down at me. One made a sign in the air.

Captain Sarros stood suddenly there. He made the same sign.

The coldness left me. I smiled up at him. "Thank you for your hospitality," I called to him. "I am not ungrateful, but I think I have found a faster means of getting to Tamarok."

He made the sign again. "It is probably better this way, Senjar Stone," he said. "You seem to attract bad luck."

I grinned. "It seems that way, doesn't it."

"Who are you, really, Senjar Thomas Stone? Or maybe I should ask, what are you?"

"I am a man haunted by bad dreams and followed by disaster," I told him. "But I will leave you now. Good fortune." I switched off the device that produced the noise, and silently I shot away from the ship. Too bad about the net, it had been an exceptionally good catch.

Opening the throttle, I skimmed the waves with great speed. The wind rushing past my face felt good, and the power between my legs left me exhilarated. I didn't miss the stink of fish-guts and the screams of scavenger birds.

I looked into the sky. A few fluffy clouds were forming ahead, they began to look like a face. In my imagination I saw the grim face of the golden man. Laughing, I shook my fist at the clouds. "Bring it on," I shouted. "I am ready!"

I passed other fishing vessels and boats, but nobody seemed to pay much attention to me.

The sky darkened, a few large drops fell, and soon it rained heavily, but it didn't matter, I was already wet from the steady spray of water that my small craft created.

A bolt of lightening parted the clouds and the thunderclap that followed seemed to be right above me.

"I am not afraid," I shouted defiantly. "You cannot hurt me. I just defeated three of your warriors."

The rain didn't last long, but dark clouds still covered the sky.

The river was long and wide. Eventually I reached a point where I could see the rising buildings of Tamarok, and after that it didn't take long until I came to the outskirts of the city. With more traffic on the river now, I slowed from my reckless speed to a more moderate pace. I could see a harbor ahead and headed for it, hoping to find transport from there to my hotel.

I never reached the harbor.

From out of nowhere two silvery sleek aircraft shot into my direction. One circled me while the other one hovered beside me, matching my speed.

"This is a closed port! Do not approach any closer!"

I felt tired, wet and irritable. I just wanted to get back on land, dry out and sleep in a comfortable, warm bed.

"To hell with you!" I yelled, opening the throttle.

"Stop immediately!" It sounded like the voice of doom. When I didn't oblige, the craft that was circling fired a string of shots in front of me, creating small geysers in my path.

"There will be no more warning shots," the voice boomed.

I got the hint. The large patrol-craft sank until it touched the water surface. It hovered beside me. A door slid open in its side and two burly Enforcers glared at me, their guns leveled at my head.

"Step aboard," one of them said harshly.

"Thank you, but I'd rather walk," I answered.

Neither of them laughed. I guess, they didn't think it was funny.

"You won't be asked again. Now move it!"

One look into their faces convinced me. I stepped across and into the interior of the aircraft. The door closed behind me with a soft *whoosh*. They pushed me into a seat and slapped magnetic bracelets around my wrists and ankles.

"Now...what did you think you were doing entering a restricted area?"

"I didn't see any signs," I answered.

"There are no signs. Let's see your identity chip."

"That may be somewhat difficult. You see, I was robbed. The thieves took everything I owned, including my identity chip."

That got a chuckle from my interrogators. "You don't look like a man anyone would want to rob. Look at that shabby coat you're wearing."

"Not mine. It's a gift."

"And the Skimmer was also a gift?" The Enforcer looked at me with narrow eyes. "Where did you get that Skimmer from?"

"I borrowed it." I glared at the Enforcer. "I didn't know this area was restricted. You cannot hold me, because I haven't broken any laws. I am not a citizen of Eden's Gate."

"We'll find out soon enough who you are. In the meantime...consider yourself in custody."

There were no windows in the cabin, but I knew the aircraft was speeding across the city toward a destination I could only guess. The slight vibration I became aware of ceased. We had landed. The door slid open and my two captors forced me at gunpoint to leave the craft.

A couple of grim looking black-clad men greeted us. They hustled me across a yard full of parked aircraft into a tall, gray building. I didn't see a sign above the door, but it was obvious this was a police station. After walking down a long, narrow corridor, we ended up in a large room full of desks and men. We stopped in front of one of the desks. They forced me into a seat, again, but this time without the restraining bracelets.

"Process him," one of my new companions told the Enforcer at the desk, then both men walked away.

I looked at the person across from me, to my delight a woman, and smiled, "Hello, it gives me pleasure to meet you. This is all an unfortunate misunderstanding. I'm sure we can straighten it out right now."

Chapter Twenty-eight

They sat on one side of the huge desk, I on the other.

One woman, two men. Neither of them much into smiling. Between us hovered the three-dimensional image of a naked man having intercourse with an equally naked woman. The image was large enough for the man's face to be recognized.

Mine.

The woman was Dorles Rodrego. Her shapely bottom moved fiercely underneath the man who wore my face.

For the third time now they made me watch the performance.

The couple changed positions. Now the woman knelt on the floor, arching her back to push up her buttocks. Moving into position behind the woman, the man put his erect penis between her slightly spread thighs, pushed forward.

The picture appeared quite clear, and the sound effects that came with it loud and very audible.

Accepting the man's penis, my penis, Dorles Rodrego moaned loudly and began to rotate her hips. The man grabbed the woman's long hair with one hand, pulled back sharply, exposing her white throat. A knife suddenly appeared in the man's right hand. With a vicious motion he drew the knife across the woman's throat, spraying crimson liquid onto the white carpet.

"You want to see it again?" asked the female Enforcer.

"I told you the first time, that is not what happened," I said, slowly losing my patience.

"You deny having intercourse with Senjarina Rodrego?"

"No, I don't. But I didn't kill her."

"We can watch it again."

"You can show this manufactured piece of so-called evidence a million times, it will not change the facts. Senjarina Dorles Rodrego was alive when I last saw her. If anyone committed a crime it was the Senjarina, who had me taken into the backwoods of your hospitable planet and left to die."

"Senjar Stone, if that is your real name, why don't you give up playing this charade." The fat, bald Enforcer who sat to the left of the woman spoke softly, but his small eyes were cold and piercing. "We compared the recording with the information in our scanners. There is no doubt; you are the man in the recording. You murdered Senjarina Rodrego."

"The hell I did! I am an innocent man. Someone wants to frame me." I raised my voice just a little. "I demand to see an attorney."

"I am the equivalent of an attorney," the fat man said.

"So why aren't you defending me?"

He spread his thick fingers on the smooth desktop. "I have no reason to defend you. It would be a waste of time. The evidence speaks for itself. You are guilty."

"Just like that?"

"Just like that." He nodded. "You are a cold-blooded killer, and you deserve the harshest sentence for this loathsome crime. I recommend twenty years in the diamond mines. Your mind will not be wiped, that would be too merciful. We want you to be aware every moment of your sentence that you are being punished." He looked at the third member of the team, a tall, thin man with a hooked nose and a bushy mustache. His black eyes stared at me out of deep sockets. "Do you agree?"

"I agree," the thin man said, his voice flat, emotionless.

"Twenty years!" I shouted. "That is over Thirty Standard years. I'll be an old man before I'm released."

The female Enforcer laughed dryly. She looked like a vulture ready to devour me. Where did they dig up these ugly and menacing looking people?

"Not many survive the mines," she said, "and the ones who do don't care if they live or die." She leaned forward. Her pale eyes were tiny pools of ice in the frozen landscape of her face. "Who hired you to assassinate Senjarina Rodrego? Tell us, and maybe we can reduce the sentence."

"Nobody hired me."

"What exactly are you doing on Eden's Gate?" the fat man asked.

"As I told you before, I am a merchant. I came here to buy spices, diamonds, and anything else I might be able to sell again, at a profit."

"We checked you out, Senjar Stone. It is true, you did make a purchase at the Intergalactic Spice Company; a large purchase, and the goods have been loaded onto your ship. Everything seems to be in order, on the surface, but we dug a little deeper. The ship you own used to belong to a man from Takkara, a planet in the Anteres System. He and his wife disappeared a couple of years ago. So did his ship." The small, cold eyes of the fat man bored into mine. "And here you are, Senjar Stone, proud owner of a vessel that has been reported missing."

"I bought it, and paid for it." I said.

"The records say you did, but did you really? Records can be tampered with. Another interesting fact…the account you are drawing your funds from has only recently been opened in your name."

"That is privileged information. You have no right to snoop into my private affairs." I said sharply.

To my surprise, he did know how to smile. It didn't make him look any friendlier. "Really, Senjar Stone. Do you truly believe that there is such a thing as privacy and privileged information?" He shook his head. "You surprise me."

"So you found out that I am a wealthy man. It is not a crime to be wealthy."

"You are correct, it isn't. But, how did you become so rich?"

"I am a merchant. I buy and sell things."

"A large sum of money has been deposited to your account. We have not been able to determine the source of the money. That tells me you have powerful and influential allies, either a government, or a criminal organization. Which is it?"

I looked into his cold black eyes and smiled. "Would it matter?"

"Not really. You're either a criminal or a spy."

"I am neither. The only reason I came to your planet is business."

"What kind of business?" It was the thin man who shot this question at me. "Why are you flying the colors of the Red Hawk Planetary System? Are you a pirate?"

Throwing my hands up, I leaned back into my seat and closed my eyes. "I am done talking. Whatever I tell you, you won't believe it anyway. I've already been found guilty." I opened my eyes and stared at them. "And another thing, turn off that damn light. If it is supposed to intimidate me, forget it, it doesn't work with me. I am going to say it just one more time: I did not kill Senjarina Dorles Rodrego."

They pushed back their chairs at the same time and got up. "We'll be back, Senjar Stone," said the woman. "Maybe you should search your memory; you might find the truth in there."

I didn't answer, it would have been a waste of effort.

After they left a couple of burly Enforcers took me back to my cell. I lay down on the narrow hard bunk and tried to catch some sleep. Waning daylight filtered into my cell through a small barred window. It would be dark soon. If I were to escape, it would have to be tonight.

Dusty cobwebs in the corners told me that this cell was not used regularly, it seemed to be in a neglected part of the building. If they put me in here for a longer stay, they might just let me starve. Until now, nobody had bothered to ask if I was hungry. I just might be able to get away without a problem. I ruled out the window as my way out of here, any tempering would trigger an alarm. That left the back wall.

These idiots were so confident; they hadn't even bothered to search me for any concealed weapons. I still had my combat knife in my boot.

I guess I fell asleep. When I opened my eyes, it was dark in my cell. There wasn't any light coming in through the small window; only a dimmed light in the hallway illuminated part of my cell.

Time to make my move.

Sliding my knife out of its sheath, I set the controls to high-density. It glowed softly in the darkness. I wasn't worried that it may fail before I was through. The power core in the hilt was indestructible and without limits.

It didn't produce any noise and no betraying odor as I slowly sliced a neat circular hole into the concrete wall, just large enough to let me crawl through. When I was finished I gently pushed against the round plug, felt it slide forward, then it plunged to the ground outside. Sticking my head through the opening, I discovered the paved ground only a meter below me. I also discovered that I looked into a back alley.

The Gods of Escape were smiling at me, after all.

I didn't waste much time pondering my good fortune. Snaking through the hole, I let my hands touch the ground, and then I pulled the rest of my body to freedom.

As I rose to dust off myself I heard a skittering noise behind me, but it was just a small animal, startled by my sudden appearance.

The concrete plug was heavy, but I managed to lift it back into place, hiding the hole from a casual observer. The more time I had before they discovered my escape, the better my chances to get away.

Of course, I had absolutely no idea where I was. I needed to get back to my hotel, clean myself up and change into some new clothes. I also needed to get in touch with Sharina and Kabrina; by now, they must be growing quite anxious not knowing what happened to me.

But they were big girls; they could take care of themselves.

None of us could foresee that we might run into any problems.

After all, we were on a civilized planet. Therefore, we did not make any contingency plans. Well, as the saying goes, hindsight is a wonderful thing. And totally useless.

I was surprised to find this alley so dark. One might expect bright lights and security cameras surrounding a police building. But then again…security measures are usually taken against break-ins. Who in his right mind breaks *into* a jail?

Breakouts were probably not common, either, with an alarm system protecting windows and doors. With any luck, my escape might not be discovered until morning.

One end of the alley was dark, most likely a dead end, but I saw light ahead the other way, and I heard noise…traffic noise. I tread my way carefully as I walked toward the light. On either side of me loomed tall buildings, their roofs lost in the blackness of the night-sky, their shadowy walls dotted by dimly lit windows. Without them, I would have been in total darkness.

I almost made it to the street, when someone stepped out of the shadows, barring my way. I couldn't see clearly if I confronted a man or a woman, I just saw a thin, tall silhouette in a long dark cloak.

"Going somewhere in a hurry?" The voice sounded reedy, young, and male. He carried something in his right hand. I registered the glint of steel.

"If you want to rob me, you're wasting your time, friend," I said. "I carry no money."

He laughed. It sounded like a dog yapping. Then he spoke to someone hiding in the darkness. "He thinks we are thieves," he said and laughed again.

Another figure stepped into view, this one short, but stocky. "Are you trying to insult us?" He had a deep, but raspy voice. "We are highly specialized professionals. We don't want your money."

"Then step aside and let me pass."

I heard a scraping noise behind me. Without looking, I knew that two more had moved into position.

"Not so fast," the thin one said.

"Alright. What do you want?" I was getting impatient. Sensing danger, the *Darkness* inside me began to gather.

"We want you!"

"Me? I am of no value to you."

"Oh, but, yes, you are. You have eyes, a heart, a liver, kidneys, blood, limbs…. You have much to give." The stocky one chuckled.

"You're probably worth more dead than alive."

They didn't see my smile in the darkness. Maybe they would have changed their minds.

I kicked backwards, felt my foot connect with a body behind me. Whirling, I brought the edge of my hand down on somebody's nose, breaking cartilage and bone. He screamed in surprise and fell to the side.

The one with the knife rushed me. His knife-arm snapped like a dry stick when I kicked it with my booted foot. From the corner of my eye, I saw the stocky one leveling something at me. I dropped, saw the flash of his gun. He didn't have time to take aim again. The blade of my knife sliced through his forearm, severing the hand that held the weapon. Stepping back, I sheathed my knife.

"Now, if you don't mind, I will take your money," I said to the thin one who stood holding his arm.

"You broke my arm and you cut off Randor's hand," he stammered. "What kind of a man are you?"

Randor let out a hoarse scream. "My hand! Where is my hand?"

"Maybe you're stepping on it," I said with cruelty. The poor bastard didn't even realize he was bleeding to death. Feeling a tinge of remorse, I told his thin friend, "Tie off his arm. Do it now, unless you want him to die."

"With my broken arm?" he whined. "Shit, it hurts!"

I sensed movement beside me. One of the other two rushed to his friend's aid. "What can I do?" he asked, looking at me.

"Take off your shirt, use the sleeve," I said.

My eyes were adjusted to the semi-darkness. In situations like this, I can see in the darkness almost as well as in daylight. This ability fades after all danger has past.

I watched him take off his shirt and wrap the sleeve tightly around Randor's arm, stemming the flow of blood. Randor stared in horror at his stump. His hand, still holding the gun, lay at his feet. "How can you do a terrible thing like this?" he said accusingly.

"You would have had no problem slicing me up," I said.

"We don't deal in body parts, just whole bodies," his friend said. He looked uninjured, but his hand went to his chest when he spoke.

I chuckled. "And that makes it alright, I suppose. Enough of this chatter. Now...all of you, empty your pockets!"

"Are you robbing us?"

"It looks that way, doesn't it? Where is your other friend?" I asked, letting my eyes sweep the alley. I saw a wooden club lying in the dirt, but no body. Then I saw the movement against one of the buildings. "Come on out," I called. "I will not hurt you anymore. All I want is your money."

The shadowy figure separated from the wall, came slowly toward me. I was surprised to see a girl, slim, of medium built. Her full breasts pushed against the bodysuit she wore. I couldn't see her face, because of her hand, which she held over it.

"You broke my nose," she said with a sobbing voice. "And now you want to steal from me?"

"Sounds unfair, I know," I said, "but you got it right. So, let's have it!"

She took her hand away from her nose, spat into the dirt. She looked a mess, blood all over her face. She probably needed reconstructive surgery.

"No," she cursed. "You'll have to take it off my dead body."

"That can be arranged," I said coldly and looked at the wooden club at her feet. That could be my unconscious body lying there. I felt no pity for her.

I stepped close to her, put my hand on her breast, squeezed hard. She cried out, reached for my eyes. Slapping her hand away, I kept mine on her breast. "Ghoul!" she hissed. "You are a Ghoul. Do you enjoy hurting people?"

"Not particularly, but I don't hate it, either, and I will hurt you more, unless I get what I want."

"Alright, you win. Just take your hand away." Her voice sounded strained because of her broken nose. It looked bad from close-up, she was lucky to be alive. I could have easily killed her when I hit her. A little harder and splintered bones would have pierced her brain.

"I've changed my mind," I said. "Keep your money…you'll need it more than I do."

It turned out that the thin, tall one had more than enough. I took most of it. Finding a taxi wasn't that hard and soon I was on my way back to my hotel.

Chapter Twenty-nine

The girls were not there. I had not expected them to be. As soon as I entered the hotel suit, and the door recognized me, a message alert flashed across the wall screen. When I activated it, the image of one of the girls materialized.

"Thomas, this is Sharina. I hope you are alright. We are worried about you. Why didn't you communicate with us? In case you didn't know, the merchandise you purchased has been loaded into the ship. We are ready to lift off. If you don't show up in five days from now we have to assume that you are dead and we will leave. Contact us when you can." She smiled. "We love you, Thomas. See you soon."

Seeing her made my heart ache. I had almost forgotten how beautiful she and her sister were. At least they both seemed to be okay, and their own business deals must have gone smoothly. Sharina made this recording just yesterday, which meant I had four days to get back to my ship.

I knew I should not waste any time, because the Enforcers would soon come looking for me, but I needed a bath badly. The smell of fish still clung to my clothing and body.

A large tub, which could be filled with scented, foamy, warm water waited for me in the bathroom. A sonic shower would have been just as efficient and much faster, but a hot bath in water is a luxury a spaceman does not have often.

The tub won.

As I sank into the bubbling liquid soft, soothing music began to play and the lights dimmed automatically.

Closing my eyes, I let the jetting streams of water caress my skin and smooth out any wrinkles and kinks that had invaded my body. Life was good, at least at this moment. There is nothing more relaxing than an old-fashioned tub full of hot, bubbling water.

Yet…something seemed to be missing to make it perfect. Without opening my eyes I said, "Computer, have an attendant sent up to my room to give me a massage…a female attendant."

"Your request has been forwarded, Senjar Stone," the computer acknowledged my order after a few moments. It didn't take long when the disembodied voice spoke again, "Attendant requesting permission to enter."

"Let her in," I mumbled, half asleep. I felt so relaxed I was almost sorry I had ordered a masseuse. I opened one eye when I heard the soft footsteps of someone coming into the bathroom.

She stood there smiling down at me. A young woman dressed in a skintight shiny purple outfit. She wore a three quarter length black coat, open in the front, revealing a nice set of breasts straining against the tight fabric of her top.

"You don't look like a masseuse," I said, opening my other eye.

"The regular masseuse couldn't come, I am her substitute," she said and chuckled. She had a beautiful smile and a pretty face. A wide belt circled her narrow waist, accentuating her breasts even more. I didn't care for the leather holster attached to it.

"Who are you?" I asked.

"I am Special Investigator Liom Valdigo. And I am not here to arrest you."

"Then why are you here?"

She laughed. "To give you a massage."

I watched her shrugging out of her coat and throwing it to the floor. She unbuckled her belt, laid it carefully on top of her coat. Then she unzipped her suit, peeled it off to reveal her naked body underneath.

Her body looked flawless, conditioned, a bit more muscular than I preferred in women, but her breasts were round and feminine. When she turned, I got a nice glimpse of her plump buttocks.

Smiling, she stepped over the rim of the tub and slid slowly into the water.

"This feels nice," she sighed and looked at me from lowered lids. She had dark-blue eyes hidden behind extremely long lashes. Her slightly curly black hair was short, cropped close to her skull.

"How did you find me this fast?" I asked.

She straightened her legs under water. Her feet scraped along my thighs.

"Where else would you go? Either here or to your ship. This was the most likely place."

"I guess I was wrong when I figured nobody would check up on me. It's only been a few hours since I made my escape."

"Normally, you would have been left alone until morning, but I had a special interest in you, and I wanted to speak to you before they moved you." She smiled. "Only I know you're gone. You have time to relax a little."

I raised my eyebrows at her when her foot touched my crotch. She had long toes, which she used expertly to wrap around my semi-erect penis. She laughed when she felt it harden under her touch. "I was told you were easily aroused," she chuckled.

"Who told you that?"

"A mutual friend."

"I see." I sat up, reached for her and pulled her closer. Her foot let go of my member as I slid her into my lap. She yelped in surprise when she impaled herself on my erect penis. "Isn't this what you wanted?" I asked and kissed her roughly. At first she struggled, but then she returned the kiss, her pelvis began to snap back and forth in my lap.

I didn't have much control in this position, so after a while I lifted her off, made her bend over the wide rim of the tub. Spreading her fleshy buttocks, I guided my member toward the puffed lips that beckoned below them. She gasped when I entered her again and pushed backwards. Her breasts were resting on the tiled rim, and I put my hands under them to get a good grip. Then I rammed myself into her with long, furious strokes.

She quivered in my grasp, cried out when she experienced her first orgasm. I climaxed inside her at the same time, but kept on going. She climaxed a couple of times before I pulled out of her.

I was far from finished.

Sitting on the cool tiles, I let her straddle me, slipped back into her hot vagina. I grabbed her buttocks and lifted her up and down. Every time she came down her feet splashed into the water behind us. Her arms were around my neck and her soft breasts pressed against me. When my fingers touched the cleft between her buttocks, she let out a soft cry.

"Be careful," she whispered harshly, "I'm a little sensitive there."

She still clung to me when I rose to my feet and walked slowly into the bedroom. Her pelvis never stopped moving. I put her down at the edge of the bed, pushed her onto her back and began hammering between her widespread thighs.

After I climaxed inside her clutching sex-organ a second time, I pulled out and lay down on top of the bed. Straddling me, she hovered for a moment, grabbed my erect penis and guided it into her hairless vagina. She sank down and sat in my lap, motionless, except for the tight walls of her sex-sheath. Slowly she squeezed them until I thought she would strangle my penis, and then she released the pressure.

"You may be the most virile man I ever coupled with," she said huskily, "but I am not without skills."

I studied her body as she sat there staring down at me. She had beautifully shaped breasts, solid and without sagging lines beneath them. When I looked closer, I saw what I had already suspected. Below each of her breasts were three barely noticeable round scars, evenly spaced.

I waited until she finished her orgasm and until her breathing returned to normal, then I said, "I know what you are."

"Of course you do. I made no secret that I am an Enforcer."

"You know what I mean."

"I don't. Tell me."

"You are Katre."

Her dark-blue eyes widened a little. Then she chuckled. "How do you know?" she asked, gyrating in my lap.

"The tender spot at the end of your tailbone, where they amputated your tail, the scars where your secondary breasts used to be, and your long toes."

She nodded, kept on moving. "I guess I should have had them shortened, too," she breathed. "But long toes are not unusual among humans on Eden's Gate. Many of them carry ancestral Katre genes."

She closed her eyes, rotated her pelvis slowly. I watched her face as she had another orgasm. She seemed to be in great pain, but I felt her hot discharge. "Now!" she whispered breathlessly. "Come inside me...now!"

I had been holding back and had no trouble obliging her. Grasping her hips, I lunged upwards, exploded with great force. Her eyes flew open, locked with mine. A deep cry escaped her open lips. My own harsh grunts seemed to echo in the room, and then it was over.

She collapsed, stretched out on top of me.

"The prophecy has now been fulfilled completely," she whispered softly into my ear.

I rolled her onto her back, entered her again. She gasped in surprise.

"You are still so hard and huge," she moaned. "Renha was right. You are not human."

"Renha is a young, romantic dreamer," I said hoarsely. "If you believe in that foolish prophecy then let me make sure you'll get enough of my sperms."

She cried out with every one of my powerful strokes, her cries turned into deep guttural growls that sounded strange coming from a human throat. She writhed underneath me like a boneless serpent, wrapped her long legs around my back and dug her heels into my buttocks.

I held back as long as I could, made her climax numerous times, then I filled her womb with my hot fluid. Whimpering, she lay in my arms, shaking in the grasp of her own orgasm. When I was finished I rolled away from her, lay on my back, listening to her loud gasps as she tried to suck air into her raw lungs.

She broke suddenly into a fit of laughter.

"What is so funny?" I asked.

"Everything," she gasped, still laughing.

"I don't understand," I said, popping myself up on my elbows.

She turned onto her side, looked at me, growled again and chuckled. "That bitch, Interrogator Francino Horras, she warned me against you, when I asked for your file. She said you are a dangerous criminal, a cold-blooded killer. A threat to society. How right she was. If she only knew how right."

"I'd like to correct you. I am not a criminal. So far, I have only defended myself against elements who meant me harm. I never kill without reason, and I don't really care about your society."

Her long fingers stroked my chin. "I believe you. You are not the threat to the humans on Eden's Gate. But your children will be."

"This prophecy. Renha told me it spoke of two sons who would be born."

Liom smiled. "Two sons and one daughter."

"What makes you so sure you are the *Chosen One*?" I asked.

"My mother, who was a seer, told me, when I was a little girl. She spoke of a stranger who will come from the stars, and who will put his seeds into my womb. I will be the mother of a warrior-goddess who will lead our people to greatness. I never believed her, but now I do."

"How can your daughter be a goddess if I am not a god?"

"But you are. No ordinary human can do the things you have done. You cannot be killed, and no prison can hold you. You walked through a wall of stone."

"With the help of a high-tech instrument. No magic there."

She trailed her fingers down my biceps, along my arm, touched my belly, then my penis. "This is the instrument of your magic. The destiny of my race lies in this piece of flesh." She put her hand on her belly. "And in this vessel, which you filled. I will protect your gift with my life."

She sat up. "I am hungry. Can you order us some food?"

"Come to think of it, I feel quite ravenous myself. I don't even remember the last time I've eaten."

Rising, she slipped off the bed, padded toward the bathroom on soft feet. Her plump buttocks quivered gently as she moved silently on muscular legs across the carpet. Smiling back over her shoulder, she said, "Order, then join me in the tub. Maybe I'll give you that back-rub you wanted."

Chapter Thirty

"By now your picture will have been flashed everywhere. You'll never make it to the spaceport without my help." Liom smiled at me over a glass of fruit-juice. I was amazed at how much that woman could eat for breakfast.

"Are you finished?" I asked.

She shook her head. "Not quite, an investigator's salary does not allow for many luxuries. I am not used to these fancy surroundings."

"Neither am I, really. Usually my quarters are less luxurious," I said.

We were both still naked. As promised, she had given me a nice body-rub, but not the way a professional masseuse would have done. Liom was a very sensuous woman, and her fingers had found every sexual responsive spot on my body. I was highly charged, sexually, and she did promise me another good workout...after breakfast.

She wiped her mouth with a napkin. Then she rose and stood looking at me from under lowered lashes, looking luscious and sexy. I had enough control to clean the dishes from the table, but then things happened fast. I bent her across the tabletop, stepped behind her and shoved my erect penis between her puffy, fleshy lips. She was already hot and moist. Flames of pleasure shot through my body as I moved my rod in and out of her tight, but soft channel. She began to whimper almost immediately and gripped the edge of the table tightly.

"Don't hold back," she moaned, "no need to be gentle. I can take it."

I will never hurt a woman when I couple with her, even if she asks me to, but I will take her to the edge.

She cried out and bucked for a long time; then I pulled out and carried her to the bed. I got between her spread legs and very slowly brought her to her last orgasm, as tremendous as my own.

Afterwards we got dressed in silence. I grabbed my belongings and we left the hotel through a backdoor.

Liom parked her vehicle in the back lane. No one saw us enter it. As she weaved her way through the traffic, I studied her profile. She was actually quite beautiful, but not that young. Even though her body looked youthful and trim, tiny lines around her eyes and mouth betrayed her.

"Why did you have your body altered?" I asked. She knew I studied her, but she kept her eyes on the traffic.

"Because I wanted to look more human," she said.

"What color were your eyes before you had them transplanted?"

She laughed and turned her head to face me. "These are my original eyes."

"I don't understand. Don't all members of your race have slit pupils?"

"Usually, but in my case the human gene was stronger. My father was human, as was my grandfather."

"But you are still considered Katre?"

Her chuckle was bitter. "Not any more, but I was before I had my tail and extra breasts removed. And before I forged my identity."

"Are your parents still alive?"

She clucked her tongue. "All those questions. One might think you are the Enforcer and I the prisoner."

"Sorry," I said. "Old habits. Tell me, what is your connection to Renha?"

"Our mothers were cousins."

"I see. I assume she is safe?"

"She is safe." Liom nodded, smiled. "She is quite fond of you. She told me to take care of you."

"So far you've done an excellent job." I grinned. "Are all Katre females as beautiful and passionate as you and your cousins?"

Liom laughed cheerfully. "Thank you for the compliment. Yes, all Katre females are beautiful, inside. The outside form is not really that important, or is it?"

I shrugged. "It shouldn't be, but I don't mind feasting my eyes on a beautiful body."

"You are shallow," she said, but smiled.

When I looked at the buildings outside I recognized some of them. We had come from the spaceport in the taxi this way. Liom changed lanes, took an exit and joined a wider highway. The buildings on either side disappeared and Liom increased the speed of our vehicle.

"When we reach the gate you keep your mouth shut," she advised me. "It is not unusual for Enforcers to visit the spaceport."

"Is there any way I could contact my companions?"

She shook her head. "Not from this vehicle. All calls are monitored."

"Too bad. By the way, there is something you need to know. I never killed that woman."

"You mean Senjarina Rodrigez?"

"I wish I'd never met her. She caused me nothing but grief."

Liom shot me a quick look. "Renha told me that you killed two Katre-Hunters, an Overseer and two guards. Even if you didn't kill Senjarina Rodrigez you are guilty of at least five murders."

She didn't know about the three Holy Warriors, and I wasn't going to enlighten her. "Not murders. I killed all those men in self-defense."

"The law won't see it that way. You are a dangerous man, Thomas, and an off-worlder. There are forces on Eden's Gate who want to stop the export of our recourses. The export companies are too powerful and control much of our economy. Off-worlders bring different and dangerous ideas, and are not welcome."

"Off-worlders also bring riches," I pointed out.

"Not to the masses. There are many poor people on Eden's Gate. The riches are only for the Great Houses." She smiled at me. "I guess by now you know that the Katre hate the humans, but they hate off-worlders even more."

"Then why are you helping me?"

She shrugged. "I don't really know, mainly because Renha asked me to." Smiling, "and maybe because of that thing between your legs."

"Not the greatest reason. I thought it was because of my charming personality," I said, grinning.

"That, too. Now, shut up. We have arrived."

Armed guards controlled the gates into the spaceport. Liom flashed her badge, and then inserted her ID-chip into the portable computer-terminal, which the attendant pushed through the vehicle's window. He didn't even give me a second glance.

Once inside the spaceport Liom grinned at me. "Security is quiet lax, because they don't expect any trouble; but those guards are very good with their weapons, and they shoot to kill."

"Who are they guarding against?" I asked.

"Katre." She couldn't hide the bitterness in her voice. "As if any of my people would ever try to board a spaceship! This is our home-world."

We parked our vehicle in one of the parking spaces assigned to visitors. "It might be best if I accompany you to your ship," she said.

"I can get you through security, they won't question my badge."

"Alright." I looked at her. "I don't want to get you into any trouble."

"Don't worry, I'll be fine."

We entered the port building unmolested. A couple of Enforcers passed us as we walked across the parking lot, but they never looked at us. Once inside the building I noticed several armed guards prowling around, but they seemed relaxed, and not very alert.

There were not many people about, and I had to remind myself that this was a spaceport, not an airport. The only travelers would be merchants and visitors to the giant space station that circled the planet.

We had no trouble getting through the security check. The guard barely looked at Liom's badge, ignored me completely. He was too busy staring at Liom's partially opened collar. I couldn't blame the man. She did have a nice pair of tits.

Soon we were walking across the tarmac toward another gate. There wasn't even a guard present when we passed through this one, just a computer-terminal, which opened the gate after Liom flashed her badge across the small screen.

On the other side of the gate, I looked around for my ship. There were a couple dozen huge transport shuttles berthed at the far end. I counted five smaller ships in berths beside one of the repair-hangars, the largest of them mine. Since we had quite a distance to walk, we took one of the service vehicles parked beside the gate.

"Are your companions on board?" Liom asked me.

I shrugged. "I hope so. There is no reason for them to hang around anywhere else."

"I suggest you take off as quickly as possible. Eventually somebody will recall seeing you pass through. And then all hell will break loose."

The girls must have been watching the tarmac, because our vehicle wasn't even close yet when the entry door to the ship slid open and one of the girls jumped down, without waiting for the steps to slide out.

She was dressed in the formfitting bodysuit common to crew. I could see the anxious and relieved look on her face. By the way she carried herself I also knew it was Sharina. When I stepped off the service vehicle, she rushed toward me and put her arms around my neck. "We were worried about you, Thomas. What happened?" she said aloud, then whispered into my ear, "Who is that woman with you? She is wearing a badge. Are we in trouble?"

I had no idea what the girls had done while we were apart, and I didn't really care to know. I patted her on the back and disengaged myself from her embrace.

"That is Special Investigator Liom Valdigo," I said. "She's a friend."

Sharina raised one eyebrow. "I see. A *good* friend?" she asked.

Liom came out of the vehicle, held out a hand. "I am Liom," she said and smiled at Sharina. "You must be one of Thomas' companions."

Sharina gave Liom an expressionless look. "I am," she said, ignoring Liom's hand.

Liom looked at me, smiled, and then she came close and kissed me. "Take care, Thomas," she whispered and turned away.

"You, too," I said and watched her get into the vehicle. She waved once, and then she took off.

"Are we ready for takeoff?" I asked Sharina and headed for the ship's entry-port.

"We've been on standby for the last couple of days," she said. "We can lift off at a moment's notice."

"Then let's do it." I climbed into the ship, didn't even wait for Sharina. I knew she would secure the airlock. Kabrina already sat at the comm-center. One thing I had to admit, these girls were efficient. I sank into the captain's chair. It was just formality. I didn't have much to do. Once I gave the order for takeoff, the ship's navigation system would take over.

Sharina took her place in the co-pilot's seat, her job as important as mine.

"Start launch sequence," I told the computer and laid my hand onto the command-terminal for identification. A soft vibration went through the ship as the fully loaded capacitors started up.

"Starsurfer requesting permission for liftoff." Kabrina spoke into her microphone and waited for confirmation from the tower.

"This is port-control," a harsh voice came over the ship's speakers. "Your request for liftoff has been denied. Do not launch. Repeat. Do not launch!"

"This is Starsurfer. What is the problem? All port-fees have been paid."

"Starsurfer, you have not been cleared. Cool down capacitors.

Wait for Port-Inspectors to board ship."

On the ship's screen I saw an official looking vehicle drive through the gate.

"What's our status?" I asked Sharina.

"We can blast off any time," she said, looking at me.

"Do it!"

The automatic system could not get us away in time, it needed clearance from the port-authorities first. Sharina overrode the computer and put the system on manual. A shiver of protest ran through the ship as we blasted off, then the equalizers kicked in, sent soothing signals to the stressed metals. Soon the spaceport appeared only as a small dot on the screen. The planet's surface curved away underneath us, and then we were looking at the huge sphere of Eden's Gate.

The planet disappeared as the view shifted and an enormous space station hung menacing in space. Moments later two small pencils broke away from the station and came streaking toward us.

"I believe they're sending a welcoming committee," Kabrina said dryly.

"Take us out of here!" I told Sharina.

Sharina worked her console with furious speed. "Get ready for the jump," she said without looking up. "They are charging weapons."

Jumping into warped space without preparations is never a pleasant experience, and I steeled myself for the onslaught of disturbing images.

They attacked me with full force, a jumble of emotions and visions, painful and unpleasant.

* * * *

Monstrous beings with giant wings and sharp talons. Millions of microscopic entities that screeched so loud that I thought my brain would fry. Hot and cold. Wet and Dry. Stormy seas. Calm, cloudless skies. Howling hurricanes. Whispering winds.

A planet in turmoil, ravaged by waves of terror.

They called her Fire-Eyes. She looked human, but her bright-blue eyes betrayed her. A transplant could have hidden her ancestry, could have changed the slit pupils into round, human ones, but those eyes made her what she was. They glowed with a terrible fire when she was angry, and she was angry most of the time.

Angry at the humans who kept her people in slavery.

She was responsible for the deaths of thousands of humans when

163

she orchestrated the destruction of a small city. She led the party of Katre freedom fighters who penetrated the security fence that kept the city safe from raiders. Many human cities erected protective fences when the uprising of the Katre began.

She claimed that she descended from a god. Together with two warlords, who had risen among the Katre people, she would lead her people to freedom. Some already called her a goddess.

Her reign was fire and destruction.

* * * *

I relaxed in my chair, opened my eyes to look at the black screen. We were alone in space.

Alone and lost.

"How far did you take us?" I asked Sharina.

She shrugged. "Far enough I hope."

"They were ready to blow us out of space," Kabrina said, giving me a questioning look. "What did you do down there, Thomas?"

"It doesn't matter. We got away, didn't we?" Kabrina smiled, her emerald eyes sparkling.

"Don't congratulate yourself too soon," Sharina said. "We've sustained damage when they fired at us."

"How much damage?" I asked.

"Don't know, yet, the computer is just running through the diagnostics."

I released the magnetic field that had kept me safe in my chair and got up. "What section received the damage?"

"One of the storage rooms got hit. Some of our food-supplies went up in smoke, but that is not the worst," Sharina said gravely. "We are in danger of loosing our life-support system. The oxygen-extractor was partially fried. We were lucky it wasn't a full hit, or we'd already be gasping for air."

"How long do we have?"

Sharina lifted her shoulders. "A couple of days, maybe three."

"Should be enough time to get us to another port. Find out where we are and locate the closest system. In the meantime I'm going to check out our cargo."

Chapter Thirty-one

The closest system was four jumps away. We could easily make it. There were four inhabited planets, none of them peopled by humans.

The atmosphere on planet number two would be poisonous, for humans, and the temperature too hot and humid.

We could breathe the air on the other three. The inhabitants were oxygen-breathers. They were even humanoid looking, but they were not human.

The life size hologram portrayed the figure of a tall biped who stood erect and proud, naked, and unmistakably male. His thin penis hung down almost to his knees. From his bald head grew a short crest that ran along his spine and ended just above his buttocks.

He displayed a handsome, arrogant face. A flat nose, wide thick-lipped mouth, and a broad chin. The eyes were completely alien, from a Human's standpoint. They protruded like the eyes of a reptile and seemed to be independent from each other. Small, shimmering scales covered the slim, but muscular body.

"How friendly are they?" I asked Sharina.

"Friendly enough," Kabrina said, "but not toward Humans. It says here, they are a warlike race."

"Do they have the capability to fix our problem?"

"They have. Apparently their technology is equal to human technology." Kabrina looked up. "We don't have much choice. We are on the outer reaches of explored human space. The *Srax* are our only chance."

"Then let's pay them a visit, but I wouldn't mind to have something to eat first."

"Neither would I." Kabrina stretched her lithe body. She looked at me from lidded eyes. "But food isn't the only thing I hunger for."

"I could use some of that myself," Sharina said and began to peel off her bodysuit.

Kabrina reached me first. She knelt in front of me, her fingers deftly undoing my belt, she pulled on my pants. Sharina pulled my boots off my feet. My penis flopped free, and Kabrina turned to present her plump buttocks. Lowering herself into my lap, she reached between her thighs, grabbed my stiff penis and fed it into her already moist sheath. Sighing, she slipped her hot vagina onto my shaft, and using the armrest of my chair she began to lift herself up and down.

She cried out softly as she experienced her first orgasm. Meanwhile, Sharina had stepped behind me and bent her head over my face, kissing me deeply. I felt the tiny prick of her needle tooth in my upper lip, registered the poison flow into my system, but I dampened it, neutralized it, without giving it a chance to affect me. We didn't have time for that now.

Kabrina lifted off to let her sister take her place. Sharina faced me, draped her legs over the armrests and took me into her. She put her arms around my neck and began to whip her bottom back and forth.

I always marveled at the suppleness of these two girls. They seemed to be completely without bones. Sharina's breasts bobbed up and down in front of my face. I bent forward, took one of the long nipples between my teeth, sucked on it.

It wasn't long before Sharina doused my shaft with her discharge. When she calmed down, I stood up, sank to the floor, with her clinging to me, and fell on top of her. Then I began fucking her with long, deep strokes. Her thighs flew wide open and she lifted her bottom to take me deeper into her. I didn't wait too long. With an animalistic roar I exploded inside her, grabbed her buttocks in a tight grip until I was finished.

When I stood up Kabrina said, with a pouting face, "What about me?"

"Next time," I said. "Now I want to eat something." When I saw the leering look on her face, I laughed and added, "I'm talking about food."

I must say, the girls stocked our food-lockers well…and with the right ingredients. The auto-cook had been programmed to prepare all kinds of fancy dishes. While Sharina supervised the process, her sister managed to seduce me again, but this time I refused to scrape my knees on the hard surface of the floor on the bridge. I saw no reason we couldn't use the bed.

I pumped between her widespread thighs until her sister called us for dinner. Then I clamped my hands around her hips and emptied myself into her violently sucking sex-canal.

Her passionate cries of pleasure were dampened by the padded walls of the bedroom. I lay on top of her soft body for a moment to catch my breath, then I rolled away and slipped from the wide bed.

"You girls will be the death of me, yet" I said as I walked naked out of the room. My clothes were still on the bridge. Sharina had already dressed and set the table in the dining room.

"I thought you two would never stop," she said when I walked into the room. "I was ready to join you, but fortunately I have more sense then either of you. I hope you didn't breathe too hard, our oxygen level has already dropped."

I grinned at her, took my seat at the table. Kabrina came in, still naked. When Sharina raised an eyebrow, she shrugged and said, "I don't have the energy to dress. Thomas took it all. First I need to eat."

We each ate a piece of broiled, fresh meat. It tasted delicious, and I didn't want to know what animal it came from. The boiled tubers, the vegetables, and the gravy were superb, and the bottle of red wine put the finishing touch to a meal fit for royalty.

"I feel like one of those ancient kings," I said, "and you two are my beautiful concubines."

They both smiled.

"We are familiar with human history," Sharina said. "We know what a king is, we also know what concubines are. How about this: Kabrina and I are the queens and you our faithful eunuch."

I grinned. "I'm afraid you don't know human history as well as you think. I wouldn't be good to you as a eunuch. Let me be the king and I'll make both of you my queens."

"Alright, as long as we both get equal time in your royal bed," Kabrina laughed.

Sharina got up. "How about you two cleaning up the table, while I go and prepare us for the jump?"

I felt like taking a nap, but I helped Kabrina with the clean-up. We put the dishes into the recycler, and then we joined Sharina in the navigation room. This time was not as bad as the last time, because the computer phased us slowly into warped space, but the visions and images never really stop completely. Usually they are quickly forgotten when you fall back into normal space. Usually, not always.

* * * *

They never told me their names, but one was a princess in her world, the other one her servant. Their beautiful, exquisite faces would haunt me for a long time. I saw two small boys, both tall for their age, both handsome. One was a prince, the other one the son of a servant-woman. Rumors said that both had the same father.

Rumors also said that he was a god. The boys grew into fierce warriors. One became a king, one a warlord. Together they conquered neighboring planets. The war in space proved terrible and costly. Enemy ships brought a plaque that exterminated half the population on the Flemlin home world. The Flemlins retaliated with weapons that should never have been used. They utterly destroyed one planet. Not even animals could survive the poisoned atmosphere. Another one left its inhabitants with a world that would slowly mutate every living being into something unrecognizable and alien.

The remaining two worlds capitulated in the face of such a ruthless enemy, became slaves to the conquerors. However, it was only a matter of time until they would rebel. There would be no peace in the star-system of the Flemlins for a long time.

* * * *

I came out of the jump sweat-drenched and exhausted.

Because of the little time we had left, Sharina programmed the computer to do all four jumps in sequence, without a rest period to let the capacitors cool down. It was hard on the ship's system, as well as ours. When we dropped into normal space, the large screen lit up. I looked at the three-dimensional image of a blue world, surrounded by three large moons.

The world of the Srax. The third planet in the system, also the largest. The fourth and fifth, which had been colonized, were smaller and conditions there were harsher than on the home world.

We didn't find too much information in our computer, since the Srax stayed isolated from the rest of the Galaxy. Fortunately, they spoke a common language on all three planets, and we did have enough words and phrases in our database to learn the basics.

We still had a few hours until we reached the planet and we used them to learn Srax.

The End, for now…

Read the exciting conclusion in Book Two, Hell's Gate
On sale now at www.melange-books.com .